ROBOTS, ROBOTS EVERYWHERE!

BOOK 2: The Robot Galaxy Series

Adeena Mignogna

ROBOTS, ROBOTS EVERYWHERE!

ISBN: 979-8-9855963-0-4 (paperback)

Edited by: Carolani Bartell

Book cover design by: Ebooklaunch.com

Published by Crazy Robot, LLC

DEDICATION

To all the robots I've ever encountered or been inspired by: big and small; simple and complex; real and imaginary.

Before We Begin

Out of the billions of galaxies and billions and billions of stars in the Universe, there was one particular galaxy that was home to only 100 thousand million or so of those stars. Out of those 100 thousand million stars or so, a large fraction of them played host to planetary systems, and while a large fraction of those had an environment suitable for life, only one species, who called themselves Humans—but who others called Umans—had still not figured out exactly how much life was going on in the rest of the galaxy.

It was not their fault, and not for lack of trying. Circumstances beyond their control, mostly to include the fact that they were in the wrong part of the galaxy, kept them fairly isolated.

Yet another star, only a mere 54 light-years from the aforementioned one, was host to a planet that was teeming with robots and one solitary human.

That planet was designated Location Zero, and the human had informed her robot hosts that her designation was Ruby Palmer.

This was a fortunate circumstance for these robots since Ruby Palmer had the ability to fix certain problems for them. One big problem in particular—they were running out of storage space.

While the robots had intended this human to help with their storage issue, this was not the issue that they were hoping to solve. The robots, one robot in particular—designated Swell

Driver—brought Ruby so they could test her DNA. Another robot—designated Detailed Historian—hoped that her DNA represented their long-lost storage.

Sadly, Ruby's DNA did not double as their storage mechanism, but her coding prowess helped the entire planet of robots, nonetheless.

Yet, while Ruby had been kidnapped, this whole circumstance was fortunate for her as well because she was now destined to become one of the most famous humans of all time—the one who had first contact with aliens—instead of potentially suffering a random asteroid hit when she tried to make her way on her own, underpowered ship, *Apple Pi*, to the new colony on Titan.

Now if she could only return to her home star system, host to her home space station—designated Astroll 2—and solve *their* problems as well. Only, she wasn't quite sure if the robots and their planet aren't quite ready for her to leave just yet.

Chapter 1

> Ruby <

Ruby Palmer didn't open her eyes. A red ceiling light flickered through her eyelids, triggering a memory of the evening before. She pushed it away. She wasn't ready to get up yet, but every time she tried to stay away from the imagery, it poked at her. Every time the light turned off, it turned back on.

"Computer, turn that off."

Still, without opening her eyes, she could tell that her command went ignored. Ruby couldn't tell if the light somehow got brighter and more vividly red or if only her annoyance made it seem so. Red. Bright.

The memory made its way a little closer to the surface of her mind with sharper, more vibrant visuals. She saw her new friend, Swell Driver. Swell Driver was a robot, which was remarkable because it was only a month or so ago that the thought of having feelings of friendship for any kind of robot was beyond Ruby's capacity or interest.

But after a few weeks in this alien world full of robots, she had gotten to know a few, and they weren't all bad. In fact, some were pretty good. Some were funny and insightful. Kind, even.

The light. The memory of noodling around on the software of her ship, *Apple Pi*. Other than boredom, she didn't know what compelled her to start noodling the previous evening. But noodling turned into finding a staged piece of software which quickly turned into a dedicated project.

Similar to her communicuff—a device she wore around her wrist most of the time—her ship was scheduled for a software upgrade. Before she left Astroll 2, she managed to avoid its installation. Ruby knew that she would lose that battle eventually. Milo Jenkins—the hanger chief responsible for keeping the ships in up-to-date working order—probably knew that, too, which is why he kept the software upgrade in *Apple Pi's* digital holding area.

As Ruby let her sleepy haze dissipate, she remembered what compelled her to look at *Apple Pi,* to begin with. Curiously, she searched to find out if the AI component of *Apple Pi's* pending software upgrade was similar to what now inhabited her communicuff. Generally, she wanted to know if there were any more parallels between the AIs created by human-kind and these robot aliens created by... well, who knows? That was one of the greatest mysteries for these robots. They didn't know who created them.

Ruby didn't know her creator either. Well, she knew her mother and was quite fond of her in the time that she was alive, but neither she nor any human knew about their ultimate creator. But that fact didn't lessen the search. It only enhanced it. The robots were no different.

Ruby opened one eye. Light. Bright. She opened the other side. Still bright.

"Computer?"

She remembered that this was not how they talked to computers here. She made a mental note to change that, but one thing at a time.

Ruby slowly sat up in bed. She was mostly used to the gravity of the robot's homeworld by now. After living most of her life on a half-G space station named Astroll 2—located in the asteroid belt of her home solar system, also home to Earth and every human she ever knew—she was slowly getting accustomed to feeling her feet constantly dragging towards the ground. The sensation was not dissimilar to Earth's gravity.

In the two short weeks she'd been here, the robots provided

her with several things to help her adjust. They managed to construct a mattress—made from a finely shredded polymeric material that Ruby swore was a simple plastic—so she wasn't sleeping on an entirely hard surface. They were not able to successfully create a pillow out of the same stuff. No matter how many attempts were made, Ruby always felt one plastic shard or another poking at her cheek. So, she continued to use her balled up jacket to cushion her head.

She still kept her MoDaC—a device not entirely different from an old-style portable computer—which she occasionally used to noodle around with computer code. But most importantly, she had her communicuff, and she'd been training its embedded AI.

Ruby initially resisted installing the AI, but her homesickness was somewhat satisfied by talking to the computerized piece from her original world. She found herself relating to her communicuff and feeling comforted by its conversation, no matter how procedural. If Ruby could travel back in time and tell herself that she would emotionally relate to an AI from Astroll 2, she wouldn't have believed herself. But she also wouldn't have believed that she'd be on a robot, alien planet.

"Pippa?"

She had left the communicuff on the table before crawling into bed the evening before.

"I'm here. Where are you?" it responded.

"Over here. In bed. Can you turn that blinking light off?"

"No, I'm not connected to the systems here yet. Remember, it's been on your to-do list for three days, seven hours, and twenty-four minutes."

"Oh," replied Ruby. She should have remembered, but her brain wasn't quite awake yet. She breathed in and out, preparing herself for the laboriously simple task of getting out of bed. She slowly swung her legs over the side of the bed and let her feet connect with the floor.

She stood, made her way across the room to the computer console, and hit a switch that stopped the blinking light.

"Ruby?"

"Yes, Pippa."

"Just checking that you're still there."

There had been curious side effects from installing the AI upgrade this far away from Astroll 2 station. The AI expected to be connected to the station and was quite disturbed that it was on its own. It had instantly developed a form of abandonment complex and frequently lamented its loneliness.

It had no other computers or AI to talk to, so Ruby had to constantly reassure Pippa that it was not alone.

Ruby promised Pippa that they would figure out how to connect it to the computer console in her cabin, giving it more access to the systems of this planet. Still, it required her to learn a little more of their programming concepts so she could write an API—an application programming interface. The robot planet end of that interface was the uncomplicated part. Pippa's own interface was a little more challenging.

But first, she needed to pick up where she left off the night before examining the software from *Apple Pi*.

She had transferred that software into a sandbox holding area—a space to safely execute a program because it was cut off from everything else—on her MoDaC where she could unpack and examine it without installing it. Luckily, the tools she kept on her MoDaC included a decompiler, which she had a lot of experience with. She was also literate in some of the common coding patterns typically used by The Company, the named owners of Astroll 2, and creators of this AI—or at least the ones who hired the consultants who created it. They were a few steps up the ladder from actually creating it, but they still got the ultimate credit.

After reconstructing some of the base code, she dug into the location services, hoping she could port it to Pippa. She needed Pippa to have a sense of place within Location Zero. Then Pippa would have the ability to comprehend being in a particular location, like Ruby's bedroom. This way, once Pippa was connected, Ruby could ask for a light to be shut off, and Pippa's location services could allow her to decipher which light Ruby was referring to instead of turning off all of the lights in the system or one random light in another room.

She sifted through blocks of code, nested together to create algorithms, passing bits of data between each, trying to find something that would be useful to her. What she saw... didn't make sense. After a while, sleepiness overcame her, so she promised Pippa, and herself, that she'd continue to work after waking up and having her morning tea.

The robots had created a facsimile of green tea for Ruby. It tasted more like bitter apple cider, but it had the caffeine kick she needed to get her brain moving.

She had accidentally stepped into the limelight of fame and admiration after helping the robots implement a data compression algorithm, saving them petabytes upon petabytes of storage space around the planet. The robots fawned over her and provided her with nearly anything they were able to construct. Or at least they tried based on the materials they were able to access, which were primarily the raw elements straight off the Periodic Table. With few exceptions, they didn't have access to any of the rich, complex, carbon-based organic materials humans cherished. Her morning tea was one of these things they attempted to produce from molecular scratch—which took a reasonable length of time and numerous taste tests that ended in spit-takes.

Ruby pressed the button on the contraption that dispensed a mug—made out of a material akin to ceramic—and began to fill it with the sour but strangely soothing liquid.

She picked up the mug, blew on it, and took her first sip as she settled into a squishy chair they had designed for her human comfort, made out of the same plastic shards as her mattress. It was custom-made to fit her height and position her perfectly at the table that her MoDaC rested on.

She nudged the computer to wake. It didn't need the caffeine like she did. It responded instantly.

As the holoscreen formed into an image with words she could read, it blinked red. Oddly enough, red was a color that the robots couldn't 'see' with their standard sensors.

Ruby placed the mug on the table.

"What the…" she said to herself.

She leaned in closer to the screen, puzzled by the odd, red blink. Her eyes drifted across the screen as 'new message' notifications buzzed. Before she could investigate the blinking, she had to dismiss the messages that came in for her while she slept. As a de facto celebrity, she received more than a hundred messages a day from robots around the planet. Most of them were simple thanks for what she did for them. Many had personal accounts, quite literally, with the amount of data they had locally and all the numbers on their specs.

These messages also came with additional promises of the things that they could do for her—everything from recreating her favorite objects of her childhood to decorating her quarters to solving complex math equations. The math equations confused her at first. This was until one of her new robot friends, Disto, explained that the ability to process advanced math equations were not algorithms every robot possessed, so offering this gift was a common custom.

Ruby usually attempted to reply to each message with a short, 'thank you' or 'you're welcome,' but it took time. She didn't have any at the moment.

After going through the messages, Ruby used her finger to select the blinky red to give her more information on what occurred with her sandbox'd code execution while she slept.

The window that popped up was a log from her attempt to run the software in the sandbox right before falling asleep. Similar to Pippa, this log contained complaints about the lack of network connectivity and the impact to location services. But there was something else.

It was a log of location predictions—the ship's location along a possible trajectory at each second. It appeared that a parameter was hardcoded—permanently built-in—to the software, which assumed that the ship's location range wouldn't extend far beyond the moon's orbit about Earth. Anything further than that would be wrong. At first, it wouldn't be too bad, but after a little while, the errors would build up, and… *it would go significantly off track!*

Ruby looked at that again to ensure she was interpreting what she saw correctly. She looked again. And again. There was no doubt in her mind. Every single ship that installed this upgrade was going to get lost in space.

Ruby leaned back in the plush chair and sipped more of the tea to make sure her brain was also processing this correctly. *Is that right?* She thought to herself. She thought through the whole thing. This software had to have been thoroughly tested. Every patch or upgrade, especially to the ships, was *thoroughly* tested. That's what The Company told everyone.

Ruby realized she didn't know what 'thoroughly tested' actually meant. She had the same level of trust as others did… it was expensive for The Company to lose a pilot. It was *more* expensive to lose a ship. The Company was known for protecting itself against even the slightest financial loss.

She had to be sure. She cloned the sandbox she created on her MoDaC and set a clean copy of the code to run, this time accelerating the processing speed.

Yes, this software was a dangerous thing. She needed to warn everyone back at Astroll 2. She needed to warn Milo.

It had only been two weeks since the day she decided to pack up and leave Astroll 2. Most, if not all of the ships would be getting the upgrade about now. The plan was to upgrade the station first, and that should certainly have been complete by now. The ship roll-out was only a matter of time.

She needed to get back. If they could send a message, she would do that, but while the robots had the ability to travel at a speed that approximated faster-than-light, they couldn't do the same thing with communications messages.

They were oddly imbalanced that way.

Yes, she needed to go home. A conflict had already been building inside her about returning. It gnawed at her that her family didn't know where she was and probably thought she was dead. She needed them to know she was okay, but she also felt some shame at running away in the first place. Although look where it got her.

Ruby had sent an audio-only communication using the robot's long-range communication equipment, but there was no guarantee it would be received on the other end. It would likely be dismissed as background noise, gibberish, or even fake—a cruel joke someone was playing on a grieving family. Ruby wanted to get back home and prove in person that she was alive and well and apologize for any distress she caused.

She took a little comfort knowing that they wouldn't have found any remnants of her ship, and maybe the lack of debris would give them hope that she was still alive. Even the concept of them having to hope that she was still alive made her shudder with guilt.

But now, she needed to get back home immediately and warn them about the bug in the location services on the software upgrade. Or else…

Well, Ruby didn't want to think about the *or else*.

She used the tattoo on her wrist to log into the robot's computer console. The robots promised her that the tattoo was temporary, and it was finally starting to fade over the course of the last week.

Ruby was, in fact, given two tattoos. The one on her right wrist was painted over a small birthmark that altered the tattoo pattern and gave her access to the deep, dark web of this world. She tried not to access it too much. Ruby didn't want to get involved in the affairs of these robots and their problems any more than she already had. She used the 'legit' tattoo one to log in.

She was starting to compose an 'I need to see you/come here now/I need help' message to Disto when there was a knock at the door.

"There is a knock at the door, Ruby," Pippa said.

"I heard it."

"I am simply trying to be helpful and useful," Pippa said in a lowered volume, almost inaudible.

Ruby wondered if Pippa understood her eye roll as she made her way to the door and pushed the button on the side console. The door slid into the wall, and Disto didn't wait for more of an invitation to roll himself inside.

"Ruby, we have a problem."

"Good morning," Ruby said in one of her many attempts to try and train these robots to have some manners. Once again, not something she actively tried to do as a brooding teenager back home. Manners were something she took for granted. But here among the robots, who had none… she had a new appreciation for them. It took a moment to mentally dial into such immersive discussions, and a simple, 'good morning,' or an apathetic, 'how are you,' was exactly the right amount of buffer time. That said, she sensed his urgency and remembered her own.

"Actually, it's early, I'm still waking up a bit, and already it's been a frustrating morning. I *do* have a problem!"

Disto's face-screen stared at Ruby for several seconds. Disto, otherwise known as Detailed Historian, was the robot that Ruby had spent the most time with and was her companion in thought. They were like cultural ambassadors to each other.

He caught on.

"Frustrating morning to you," he said. "Now, can we get on with it?" Disto asked.

Ruby thought about correcting him—telling him that it's just the thing to say whether you're having a good morning or not. But instead, she got on with it.

"I need to take *Apple Pi* and go home."

"No, no, no. That's why I'm here. Your ship. I thought our researchers were merely examining it. Instead, they've taken it apart!"

"Are you kidding me!?" Ruby's eyes went wide, and the rest of her face went slack. "First, I was told that one of your special engines was getting installed so that I could leave *whenever* I wanted to. Then I was told the technology wasn't compatible. Then, everyone decided that SD could simply drop me, safe inside *Apple Pi*, off where he picked me up when I was ready to leave. Well, now I *need* to leave." Ruby had her hands on her hips. "It's like you guys are deliberately trying to keep me here or something!"

Disto's hue turned a shade of orange that Ruby had come to recognize as the robot equivalent of a blush. In this case, it was because Disto was clearly hiding something or lying.

He rolled back and forth in the room, unintentionally simulating human pacing.

"That's no secret, Ruby. *Many* of us want you to stay."

"*Many?* But not all," Ruby said, eyes narrowed.

"Correct. It is not 100% of the robots on Location Zero."

"Well, 100% of me knows I need to go home. How do I get my ship back in order?"

"That's what I'm here for. They don't want to give you your ship back at all."

"Who is 'they'?"

"The Agency of Interfaces. They've sent an Agent for us to talk to."

Chapter 2

> Ruby <

In the makeshift hanger where *Apple Pi* sat for the last month collecting dust—because, yes, a robot planet with no naturally occurring biological organisms still managed to have dust—stood Ruby, Disto, and several other robots. Noticeably absent was Swell Driver, the robot who initially kidnapped Ruby and brought her to this place.

Swell Driver, or SD, as Ruby had nicknamed him, had not yet returned from the most recent in a series of multi-day space missions that he hadn't been terribly enthusiastic about. Ruby had some slight guilt pangs in her stomach because she knew that one of the reasons SD wasn't terribly enthusiastic was that he couldn't take his own ship. The 'hanger' that *Apple Pi* was in wasn't exactly a hanger but the belly of SD's ship. So not only did SD not want to go on those missions, but he also had to use another ship, not his own. Ruby knew how that would have made her feel had the situation been reversed.

Two of the other three robots Ruby already knew. They were Fastidious Mechanic and Testy Engineer. The third was new to her. He was introduced as Austere Agent 607 from the Agency of Interfaces, and he was the reason Disto was on edge this morning.

Well, that and the fact that *Apple Pi* was in no condition to go anywhere. As Ruby surveyed the piles of spacecraft parts scattered across the floor, she wasn't sure if it would ever go anywhere ever again. Fastidious Mechanic and Testy Engineer were also surveying the carnage. Though to them, it was not carnage but their handiwork. Ruby's brain flashed back to recent discussions she had with both of them about her ship. She thought Testy Engineer was merely curious. She had no idea he was going to use the information she provided to *disassemble* it.

"As you know," Austere Agent sounded to Ruby like an annoyed civil servant, "we do not maintain details of all the technology of every species we've encountered. It will not be possible to reassemble it without detailed documentation on the component interfaces."

And to Testy Engineer, he said, "And did you not record the disassembly process?"

By his coloring—threet-level as Ruby remembered they called it—Testy Engineer was not happy to be put on the spot. "I..."

Before Testy Engineer could stammer out any other words in his defense, Austere Agent turned to Ruby.

"You will need to provide the required instructions."

"Are you kidding me?" Ruby hadn't recognized the pitch her voice achieved as one she was capable of.

"You had no right to take my ship apart," Ruby said sternly after getting her voice back to normal. "I don't have any assembly instructions. I'm a pilot, not an engineer." She turned to Testy Engineer, who was, in fact, an engineer.

"Isn't your memory a recording device? Can't you simply remember?"

Testy Engineer looked down at the floor. His outer chassis coloring reflected shame.

Disto rolled over to him, and the two exchanged some computerized tones in their native robotic language.

Disto returned to Ruby and Austere Agent. He produced the robotic sigh that Ruby had grown fond of and accustomed to.

"He's quite embarrassed," Disto said.

"That's obvious. But it's not obvious why," Ruby said.

"His on-board storage is limited. He is not using your algorithm, Ruby. He was afraid of the update. Afraid of... alien technology."

Ruby blinked and looked over Disto to the robot that wouldn't look directly at her. Disto had mentioned a few days earlier that a handful of robots like Testy Engineer refused the update. Still, she thought that it was a rare enough occurrence on a planet of over 100 million robots that she would never meet one.

She shook her head, "I don't have time for that. I need to get home. Forget your technology. Forget my ship. Can't SD simply drop me off at Astroll 2?"

At this, Austere Agent's coloring began to oscillate between two colors that only made Ruby think of unpleasant excretions humans made when they were not well. He was looking her up and down, and if he had any salivary glands, he might have spit in her general direction. At this moment, Ruby was thankful that, to the best of her knowledge, none of these robots secreted anything—saliva or otherwise.

"Are you suggesting that SD," he paused as if it took physical effort to say what he was trying to say, "'interface' with additional Bio technology?"

Ruby looked at Disto, confused. Disto didn't look as confused but took on the color of embarrassment, then looked back at Austere Agent.

"He's done it before," she said flatly.

"You may submit an appeal to the Agency of Interfaces in accordance with the implementation instructions for Directive 11. However, the number of requests received have increased recently, and they are handled first in, first out."

"This is a joke, right?" Ruby glared at Austere Agent and took a step towards him.

"Ruby..." Disto said, but she ignored him, taking another step towards the Agent.

"You took apart my ship, I'm stranded here, and now I have to file an appeal?" Every muscle in her body tensed up, and she wanted to grab and squeeze something.

Austere Agent didn't back away but stared directly at Ruby. "You might be here with us for some time more. Stay out of trouble. Stay out of our way." Austere Agent rolled out of the hanger without saying any more.

Disto approached Ruby, and she could tell that he wasn't quite sure what to say.

"Please do not worry, Ruby," he eventually said. His primary appendage was jutting out from his chest, and it was gently touching Ruby's upper arm. Less than two weeks ago, a movement like this would have freaked her out at best and sent her into a panic attack at worst, but Ruby came to adjust to the robots' physical expressions of kindness. So, she didn't wince, or shudder, or even have a second thought when Disto brushed her arm with a cold, metal appendage and said, "We will get you home."

"I need to leave as soon as possible. I thought I could leave immediately. But this…" she waved her hands over the splayed-out equipment. She recognized her piloting console at her feet and sighed.

"It won't be today, but soon. We will make the request through the Agency of Interfaces as he suggested. However," Ruby, now that she was attuned to reading the facial expressions the robots could produce on their face-screens, swore she saw a smirk. "The queue isn't always first in, first out."

Ruby caught on. "The 88?" she asked. She knew she could say this out loud because all of the robots present were members.

The 88 was an underground rebel movement of robots that recognized the problems of their world and were working to fix them. They operated outside the hierarchy of agencies, offices, and official groups of robots that were bogged down in broken processes and procedures. What they were increasingly finding: corrupted data.

"Can you guys put this back together in the meantime?" Ruby said. She was addressing Fastidious Mechanic and Testy

Engineer. Neither robot responded.

When this happened, Ruby replayed what she said in her head, found her mistake, and asked the question in another way: "Fastidious Mechanic, Testy Engineer: can the two of you put this back together?"

Add 'guys' to the mental list of idioms the robots can't yet process, Ruby thought.

The two robots communicated back and forth in their native beeps and often ear-piercing sounds. Disto joined in the conversation before Fastidious Mechanic finally responded.

"Yes. I recorded visuals of the disassembly. We can reverse the procedure."

"I thought you said you didn't record anything?"

"No, he didn't," Fastidious Mechanic said, pointing a slim appendage at Testy Engineer. "I recorded it all."

"Why didn't you tell us this before?" Ruby asked.

"I wasn't asked."

Ruby put not just one but both hands to her forehead. She closed her eyes and took in a very deep breath, remembering who—or what—she was dealing with. She let her lungs empty completely while counting to seven in her head.

When she opened her eyes, she asked, "How long until it's back together?"

After a few more beeps between the robots, "Approximately 250,000 tics, or 2,500 clicks."

Ruby did the mental math. A tic was the fundamental unit of time the robots used, and fortunately, it was close enough to a second that she could convert in her head. A click, which was 1,000 tics, was less convenient in that way. But knowing that there were 86,400 seconds in one day, she memorized that there were 172,800 in two days, 259,200 in three days, and so forth, so she wasn't performing real math in her head, only looking it up from memory.

"That's a little less than three days," she said aloud, but more to herself, although Disto was aware of Ruby's timescale and what it meant for humans to be on a '24-hr clock.' So, Ruby looked at Disto while she said it.

"Two point nine days exactly," Disto said. "I'm sorry that I can't set my default timescale to report in your days." Ruby smiled and nodded. Disto had explained that there were many hardcoded parameters in his system. Ruby considered looking into this code to make it easier to communicate but then rethought this. While it might be good practice for her to understand how they worked, adjusting them to function under her own hardcoded parameters would be wrong. She adjusted her own programming instead.

"We can have Austere Agent's appeal submission processed in that time," Disto said, "For you to return home only. I'm afraid sending you back on your own, with our technology, will not speed up the process. None of it is accommodated for a bio-pilot. We'll have to bring you."

"And by 'we'…" Ruby folded her arms. She knew that Disto knew who she was talking about. She didn't want to say anything aloud in front of the others.

Her last conversation about SD was one of concern on both their parts. They were both equally worried about SD. At one point, neither of them would have questioned that he would be the one to escort Ruby home, but now… some other robot might need to come along.

No one said anything else.

Disto managed to produce a wink on his face-screen without saying more, and then he rolled to the door. The other two began to follow him. He turned to them, "What are you doing? You need to stay here and return *Apple Pi* to a functioning state." They looked at each other and then rolled back to the ship parts.

"Ruby? Are you going to join me? We should find SD."

"Later. I need Pippa's help to work on the computer, and it will be faster if we establish a direct connection."

Disto moved his head in understanding and continued his way out.

Before Disto left the hangar, Ruby silently observed Disto shine a laser from his neck to the ground in a series of blips that reminded her of Morse code. The other two robots each returned a blip, and Ruby made a mental note to ask Disto about that later.

While Fastidious Mechanic and Testy Engineer busied themselves on reassembling the bulkheads, Ruby made her way around to where the main computer was sitting—an unassuming box on the floor, next to other parts that were typically supposed to be inside the console. The cockpit chair was conveniently located next to it.

Ruby sat in the chair and saw that the two robots were occupied and mostly out of view, thoroughly involved in their task. She wished she could have had a little more privacy but knowing that they were members of the 88 made the situation feel secure enough. So far, the 88 proved to be quite trustworthy. Although it was odd that Testy Engineer, a member of the 88, was also a group member that feared her 'alien technology.'

"Pippa," she said into her wrist at such an angle to deliberately activate a visual interface.

The holofigure—a disembodied face in ethereal, transparent blues and greens—came to life, hovering a few centimeters above her wrist. "Ruby?" it said.

"Let's get you hooked back up to that computer. We're not going anywhere today or tomorrow." She bit her thumb and sighed, "Or the next day. But hopefully the day after that…"

She was staring at the pieces of *Apple Pi* and wanted to be more upset. Before this morning, Ruby didn't have an urgent reason to go home. Reasons, sure, but none that convinced her she should leave such an extraordinary place quickly. She had said several times that she was planning on staying for months. And when the robots asked about examining her ship, she readily gave the green light. They had asked to 'scrutinize,' she now recalled. Was 'scrutinize' a mistranslation of a word that should have come out more like 'disassemble?' She didn't know.

She reached underneath the main console, discovered that the compartment wasn't there, and remembered it was laid out on the floor. A pang in her chest, her hands reflexively fisted, and her arm tensed before she brushed off the inconvenience and sent her grasp in the correct direction. It was sealed how it always would be underneath the console. She opened it and pulled out a network cable. Ruby connected one end to her communicuff and the other to *Apple Pi's* computer.

"Do you have a solid connection to the ship, Pippa?"

"Yes indeed!"

"How is the intrusion detection system holding up?"

Pippa paused. "Which part?"

Now it was Ruby's turn to pause. "What do you mean which part? I wanted to know if anyone was entering *Apple Pi's* systems without asking... straightforward, one-part question."

"Ah! But there are multiple entry-ways, aren't there?" Pippa responded with. "So no, no one has gone in through the hatch. They took the hatch off. I would have told you about that already."

"But..?" asked Ruby. She sensed the yet unspoken 'but' in Pippa's tone.

"*But,*" Pippa repeated. "But, I activated the ship's computer intrusion system as well for both the console and wireless access."

"But no one could access the console without my biometrics, Pippa," Ruby said. Snarkily. "And they don't have any form of pur-fi comms like we do, so no one was going to access it wirelessly."

"I know they told you that," Pippa said.

"But...?" Asked Ruby, correctly sensing that there was still another 'but.'

"But, I think they provided false information. Or you pur-fi in your sleep."

"They lied?"

"Or you did something in your sleep."

Ruby rolled her eyes instinctively, confident that Pippa didn't see or understand that gesture. "Let's rule that ridiculous option out for the moment."

"Overnight, someone or something—I can't tell what it was—tried to access the ship. Wirelessly."

"They had my MoDaC for a while. Could they have used it? Or adapted the technology from it?"

"Did they have your MoDaC as recently as last night while you were sleeping?"

"No," Ruby said, remembering that her MoDaC was with her in her room. For a moment, she imagined getting up in the middle of the night and accessing the ship wirelessly in her sleep. And as far as she could remember, she never slept-walked. When she slept, she slept. Except for the vivid, felt-like-she-was there, dreams she'd been having ever since arriving. But she still slept. Yes, doing anything else in her sleep was indeed a ridiculous option.

"Right. I said *tried* to access. Tried and failed. *Apple Pi* rejected the connection attempt and logged it. If they had the MoDaC, they would have succeeded."

Ruby processed that information. She put a hand on the piece of *Apple Pi's* outer hull. It wasn't cold like it might be in the air-conditioned deck of Astroll 2, but it wasn't warm like it would be when it had been running for a while. It was room temperature and comfortable, although Ruby was not. Her face was hot, and she had goosebumps forming from the chilly, metallic room.

"They lied," she said softly to herself.

"Maybe," said Pippa. "I can compute many, many scenarios where you were not lied to, yet this still occurred."

"Such as?"

"Such as you sleep-communicated."

Ruby rolled her eyes. Again. Her eye muscles were getting a workout this morning. She wondered if Pippa could see it this time.

"Don't roll your eyes at me," Pippa said.

"Fine. Then give me a more realistic scenario."

"Someone recently innovated technology like yours and is operating it covertly."

Now that was likely. Ruby constructed a variety of scenarios that made her feel a little bit better—she wasn't lied to, but there was more going on. More than she knew. More than her mechanical friends knew. It was an immense planet with a lot of robots. She chided herself for her small thinking—that a handful of robots represented all the planet had to offer. That these robots she interacted with, even as close to the central Core as they were, could possibly know everything that was happening on this world.

This thought made her feel a little better.

And then, much worse as she understood the danger they were all in… She put the thought outside her mind.

"Let's go find SD," she said to Pippa. "It's time I catch up with him, find out about his latest trip, and see if he's in any condition to drive me home."

Chapter 3

> Ruby <

The computers told Ruby that SD was in the Inner Nonagon. The Inner Nonagon was in the physical center of the Sector, and this center was, at least metaphorically, the center of Location Zero. That is to say that she was in the regulatory hub of activity, similar to what she might find in the capital of a country on Earth.

She had spent some time learning a little about other Sectors and wanted to travel but was confined to the bubble, "for your safety," a robot from the Hall of Circulation had told her. She knew that this bubble didn't directly reflect all of the other sectors, so naturally, she wanted to see all of this for herself.

She tried to argue that she wasn't in any more danger anywhere on the planet but was given additional excuses. The best one was that long-distance travel on the planet wasn't set up for Bios.

Turns out, she couldn't argue that one. The only restroom was still located in her quarters. They would have to build one everywhere she went when she needed to pee—a reoccurring issue. The portable version that had been promised had yet to materialize.

Ruby had strolled through this large room several times over the past few weeks. It reminded her of some otherworldly version of central park, without any of the fauna. Entrances to corridors lined all of the walls—nine large walls. The center of the room contained a platform, and spaced every few meters extending out from the platform were kiosks. Each kiosk had a robot or two—or as many as four or five—plugged in.

There were even a few places where a Bio, such as herself, could sit and watch robots come and go through the large area. She often found herself peeking at the oversized screens on the walls in-between the corridor entrances, watching the flashing screens catch her up on the daily news.

But now was not a time to sit. Ruby walked around all the recently familiar kiosks, looking at all of the snowman-shaped robots. She moved swiftly as if she'd known this place for years rather than the two weeks she had actually been here. When she couldn't find SD, she climbed onto the platform. From there, she could see nearly the entire arena. And there he was. At a kiosk, by himself.

Ruby hopped off the platform and made her way over to SD, nearly bumping into a robot or two to do it. They let out a few beeps in response, but she hardly noticed as she cantered over to SD. For the first time today, she felt hopeful at the sight of him.

"SD!" Ruby couldn't help but smile.

SD didn't respond.

SD wasn't plugged into a kiosk like the other robots were. He was simply existing there, by himself. His face-screen wasn't entirely blank; its background had a greenish hue. He was, for lack of a better description, staring off into space. She raised her eyebrow and paused before deciding to step closer.

Ruby approached SD from the side and once again asked, this time with a slight lilt in her voice, "SD?"

When SD didn't respond, she reached her arm out to touch his chassis and received a mild shock of static electricity. It didn't hurt much but was enough to startle them both.

SD's face-screen took on the characteristics she recognized as she shook her arm back to normalcy. Simple graphics represented eyes and a mouth that curved into a slight smile.

"Ruby, it is nice to see you."

"Yeah, you too, SD. Why haven't you come to talk to me since you got home? You promised to take me on a tour of some of the other ships, but you just…"

SD blinked. Ruby recognized this action as trying to recall something.

While waiting for SD to speak, Ruby thought she saw an unusual robot in her peripheral vision.

"You just…" Ruby tried to finish her phrase, but her words were lost as her eyes were drawn elsewhere.

The robot was all black. Not typical in a sea of robots whose base color was typically white, off-white, beige, light gray, or a host of other light colors. But in the half-second—or half tic—it took her to turn her head, the robot was gone.

"…disappeared…" She finished the phrase as her eyes grazed the crowd for the missing robot.

She refocused on SD—her *found* robot.

"Tell me about your trip," she said.

"There is not much to tell."

"SD! You're the first and only interstellar traveler I know. You have to realize by now that even things you find unremarkable, *I'll* go nuts over." She paused and waited for him to respond, then followed up his silence with a question, "*So*…? Where did you go? What kind of stars and planets were you near? What's out there? Inquiring minds want to know."

"I continue to be amazed at your interest in space travel, Ruby. It is, well, pleasantly boring."

Ruby chuckled. "And I continue to be amazed by your relentless *boredom* of space travel."

An indicator light blinked on SD's mid-section.

"I must go," he said.

"Where?"

"I have an appointment," SD said.

"Okay, but where?"

"I shall see you later, Ruby."

SD started off in the direction of one of the openings that connected this area to a series of hallways that led to all sorts of interesting places that Ruby had been exploring over the past few weeks.

Ruby was tempted to follow SD, to maybe get some more answers to questions along the way, but sensed he wasn't going to be any more forthcoming either way.

Something else caught her eye. She caught another glimpse of a pitch-black robot from the side of her vision. It was moving off, but in the direction opposite SD, to another hallway entrance. This time, as Ruby trained her eye on it, noticing that it had a large blueish dot in the center of its topmost chassis.

She moved to follow it, but she couldn't tell which way it had gone by the time she reached the hallway entrance. From her vantage point, she could see at least three different paths it could have chosen.

While Ruby was figuring out what to do, her stomach grumbled, making the decision for her. It was time to eat.

> Ruby <

Ruby arrived back in her room long enough to put in a meal order before the door chime rang. She was about to use the waiting time to quickly use the bathroom facility that the robots installed for her before doing additional research but answering the door had bumped its way up in the order of things to do.

Ruby walked over to open the door, and after it opened with its usual *swoosh*, Disto rolled in.

"The request is in," he declared confidently. "And maybe the request has been in for two weeks. Wink, Wink."

"Did you just say 'wink, wink' out loud?"

"Yes, it is much easier to say than to do, and there is a higher probability of your hearing the gesture than seeing it, especially since you're not looking at me. What are you doing?"

Ruby had already moved back to the console and touched the screen to wake it up, forgetting her other biological needs that were suddenly less urgent.

"Getting ready to eat. But more generally, I think I'm still learning more about your world," she said, shaking her head gently back and forth. Disto was always a better source of information than searching the robot's computer system anyway. Ruby turned to Disto to give him her full attention.

"Can you tell me: What do you do when one of you is sick?" asked Ruby. "Are there doctors? Mechanics?"

"We have the Office of Reductions. I presume you are using the biologically applicable term, 'sick,' as an analogy to mean malfunctioning. The Office of Reductions takes our functional problems and makes them smaller problems."

Ruby wondered, *the problem won't be solved? Only lessened?* She squinted, "I don't see how that fixes you. Will it help SD?"

Disto shook his head. "In this case, I fear they would take him apart."

Ruby fell silent. When she didn't speak, Disto offered, "Did you see him today?"

Ruby nodded. "And he's simply not himself. I can't describe it. If he were human, I would say he's sad or melancholy. We have doctors for that sort of thing."

"Ah!" Disto declared. "He needs to visit the Rejuvenation Region 1010."

"The *what?*"

"It's a place where robots can work out their issues. When they aren't having technical problems, but problems like you describe. When they get what you'd call...*depressed.*"

"Robots can get depressed?" Ruby asked, cocking her head to one side.

Disto explained, "Not in the way your species do, since we do not have the myriad of chemicals transmitting messages between our internal components. It's a form of mechanical discombobulation. An imbalance of electronic signals which affects communication, motor, and decision-making abilities. This mismatch of circuits can result in delayed response time but could also cause a robot to cease its ability to process any input data—effectively becoming inert. Rejuvenation Region 1010 has the processes and procedures to restore a robot who experience this phenomenon back to a functioning state."

"Are they... comfortable? The procedures, I mean." Ruby asked.

Disto answered, "They vary from procedure to procedure. They range from rather relaxing to magnanimously disorienting. The few I've known who have gone to Rejuvenation Region 1010 have not done so on their own accord. Because—"

Ruby interrupted, "Because a robot in that state wouldn't necessarily have the initiative to go due to their electronic imbalance, nor would they want to experience the uncomfortable processes involved. Right?"

"Right." Disto said, "You grasped that concept quickly."

Ruby shrugged, "Look. Like you said, it's equivalent to humans. SD won't want to go or might not even think that he needs to. So, what? We file some sort of request and get him admitted?"

"It's not that simple, Ruby. This sort of malfunction is considered low priority as it can sometimes rebalance over time. Unless there is clear evidence of an individual's primary directive being neglected, behavioral misconduct, or some sort of clear and complete malfunction...SD has to volunteer."

Ruby considered whether or not she could persuade SD to go. Of course, for that to work, she'd first have to convince him to speak with her for more than a few minutes without running off.

She searched her memory for what she knew about these places on Earth and came up empty. Her knowledge came from media, not real life. There was the place her grandmother was in, but it wasn't any sort of rehab; it was a permanent facility for the elderly who needed special care. Uncle Blake told her the story of how she also did not go voluntarily, but she knew it was permanent, not temporary.

Then her memory sparked.

"If I can speak to him, I think I can convince him to go," Ruby said. "You said this is equivalent to human depressions, right? In my biology class, we had to learn a little about psychology. I think I have a few ideas of how to convince him. And after all, I'm probably just going to be sitting here waiting for a day or two. So, where's the rehab place?"

Disto's coloring turned optimistic.

"It's on Level 1, but in the next sector, Playfully. By the time you're back, I'm sure we'll have everything in place to send you and *Apple Pi* on your way," his demeanor quieted, "although I wish you didn't need to leave so abruptly."

"I need to get home, Disto," Ruby said. She proceeded to catch him up on the problem she found. Until she felt a pang in her lower abdomen.

"I was actually about to take care of some of my biological functions when you came in," Ruby said dryly. "I still need to go do that." She wasn't going to re-explain all of this to Disto.

In her first few days on this planet, Ruby had spent a great deal of time explaining her basic biological functions and needs to Disto and several other robots. This involved correcting a lot of misinformation they had on her species.

While the robots had known and been in touch with other biological organisms such as herself, it had been a while, possibly years, since any had been present on their planet for any duration that would require the robots to know much about their needs.

The robots were accommodating and built a bathroom that was almost luxurious by the standard she was used to on Astroll 2.

At first, she had been able to make use of the facilities on *Apple Pi* but was grateful once she no longer needed to visit her ship every time she had to pee.

But Ruby clarified to her robot hosts that if her quarters now contained the only compatible bathroom—or biological waste facility as the robots called it—she couldn't go too far away.

The robots promptly agreed they would build a mobile version for her, but one had yet to be produced.

"Ruby?"

Ruby blinked. She had been caught, lost in thought, once

again.

"Sorry, what were you saying?"

"SD. You need to bring him to the Rejuvenation facility."

"Level 1, Playfully Sector, you said?" Ruby learned that the robots divided regions—regularly defined by latitude and longitude on a planet's surface—into sectors whose names translated into adverbs. They were currently in Mortally Sector. Besides the unusual naming convention, the other interesting thing that Ruby learned about the sectors was how they were firewalled from each other.

"That is correct," Disto replied. "It is good to see that your memory facility is still intact."

"Why wouldn't it be?"

Disto looked uncomfortable for a moment.

"I was thinking of another biological species," he said. "They are called the Clasuoids. Their memory degrades anti-asymptotically as they near the time to relieve themselves. It is not uncommon for them to forget when and where they need to do so. It results in a lot of... accidents."

Ruby saw the opportunity and bolted out of the chair. "Well, then how do you know that's not going to happen to me? I need to pee, and my food will be here soon." She found it funny that this tidbit of information that was the thing that made Disto finally understand the importance of her biological needs. She refocused, "SD told me he had an 'appointment' but not where or with who. I'll go check his enclave after I eat."

Disto turned towards the door.

She stopped him, "Actually... wait here while I go to the bathroom... I want to ask you some more questions."

Disto made a soft tone that Ruby knew meant "sure thing." She smiled and continued onto what was now a mad dash for the bathroom.

Chapter 4

> Detailed Historian <

Disto watched Ruby walk into the personal waste reclamation facility. He had received a report on how much was reclaimed from this human... disappointingly, the majority of it was made up of atoms that organics used. A lot of water, so a lot of oxygen and hydrogen. A lot of carbon. A lot of nitrogen, too.

Disto knew that a plethora of processes were being followed to prepare and distribute the various elements to places on Location Zero that could put it to use. Some of it was remixed into the air that was not only breathable by Ruby and most of the other biologicals but also some of this matter was involved in new construction.

There was a historical reason for the atmosphere kept inside Location Zero.

Location Zero was small by planetary standards but a large pain in the lower chassis by management's standards. There were so many systems to keep running, and robots that focused on the 'why' of everything were not much use for completing tasks.

Disto was in between logic processors on that issue. On one appendage, the historical context was important, and most robots agreed that figuring out what happened to their long-lost data storage was an important thing.

On the other appendage—since Disto had two—most robots on the planet had more immediate concerns.

While waiting for Ruby to finish with her immediate biological needs, Disto rolled over to the computer console and accessed his personal correspondence space.

These days, he was overwhelmed by the volume of communication he received. He couldn't keep up. It had been this way ever since his association with Ruby was revealed.

Robots from all over Location Zero wanted to communicate with him. Mostly to offer their version of a thank you. Disto appreciated this. Some were outraged that he associated with a Bio. Disto did not appreciate that. Some didn't know why they were contacting him other than to say that they sensed they should, given their closest enclave-mate had made such a big deal about it. Disto calculated the amount of time wasted by those.

Disto didn't have any advanced skills with the computers, but as someone who specialized in information, mostly of the historical variety, he was generally more well versed in the tools used to sort through information—at least more than the average robot.

He set up a series of filtering rules to move the majority of these messages to a less intrusive place.

What a waste of space! Even with Ruby's compression algorithms, freeing up a lot of space for data, he wished that individual robots would take more responsibility for their data and not waste it.

He skimmed through the filtered-out messages. Most could be deleted. He selected all of them, and right as he was going to key in the command to permanently delete them, the first few words of one particular message caught his eye.

It said, 'Dangerous paradoxes revealed. May I have your attention, Disto…'

It was from another member of the 88. Only members of the 88 wrote poetically cryptic opening lines in communications. A circuit activated inside him. Outwardly, if someone saw him, they would see his color turn a little more than one threet—slightly less than the standard two—enough that anyone who saw him would recognize the hue of his excitement. Ruby was not yet out of the waste chamber, so he took control of his coloring.

He transferred the message someplace where he could review it later and permanently deleted the rest. Even though these messages weren't hosted on his local storage, deleting them made him feel lighter.

He sighed.

That was when Ruby re-appeared.

"Are your systems fully evacuated?" Disto asked.

Ruby scrunched her nose. She said, "Yeah, but I don't think I'll get used to being read aloud an analysis of my pee and poop as it's happening," she said.

"We can turn that feature off if you'd like," Disto replied.

Ruby looked up at the part of the room that was in between the wall and the ceiling. Disto recorded that she did this often. He recognized this to mean 'I must process this information. Let me be for a tic or two.'

After three tics, Ruby said, "No, it is… interesting." She returned to the chair next to Disto.

"Do you know where those atoms are destined?" she asked.

Disto was confused, "As I told you the other day when I was present for your bodily excretion activity, I do not have access to that specific information. The raw materials are shipped to one of several processing facilities on the planet. There is an interconnected chute system located a few levels below us that is responsible for transport of all materials and equipment throughout the planet."

Today, she shrugged her shoulders at this. But the other day, he had asked her what was so interesting, and she responded that it was another way for her to learn about the planet.

Both Disto and other robots recorded Ruby spending a significant portion of her time absorbing information from her computer console. Once, Fearless Communicator was present and had asked:

"How much is your own onboard storage?"

To which Ruby had replied, "I don't know. We don't—we can't—calculate it like that. Most humans believe that our memory is some kind of dynamic, elastic muscle." She paused, and the surface of her face formed another expression that Disto associated with the inability to recall additional information. She added, "I know I've always been good at remembering things I read."

Disto was later informed that this bit of information was communicated around and made its way over to Agents at the Agency of Process Improvement, who were so excited by the idea that they kicked off a whole new project within their agency to see if they could devise new storage mechanisms based on this concept of elasticity.

Ruby had inadvertently sparked a lot of interest and passion for new projects, new ideas, new ways of thinking.

But all the newness remained overshadowed by the existence of so many problems that, if not resolved, would impede any progress in any area. Disto understood why Ruby expressed an urgent need to return to her own home but wasn't ready to see her leave and hoped that after her own emergency was abated, she would return.

At that, a beep chimed on the door.

"Lunch!" Ruby called out, popped out of her seat, and allowed the door to swish open.

A robot carried in a tray, left it on the table, and excused itself without saying anything. Ruby shouted, "thank you," at it as it rolled away.

"What did you order today?" Disto asked.

"I wanted to be a little adventurous." Ruby waved her hand over the tray that contained several small dishes of food stuffs. None of it would have been recognizable as food to anyone back home, visually, but the robots had been able to replicate the taste and nutritional content that met Ruby's needs. "I'm still amazed at how Bitter Packager is able to create this."

Disto was, too. While he had some passing knowledge about the foodstuffs that biological organisms required, he had never met a Packager, a robot who was responsible for creating those foodstuffs, before.

Bitter Packager had shown up one day to scan the inside of Ruby's mouth—what she called the orifice on her head that was responsible both for communication and ingestion of foodstuffs—and explained how it would help in the replication of any taste she described.

For the first few days, Bitter Packager delivered the food himself, ensuring that Ruby found resulting tastes to be accurately represented. His mood for the rest of the day hinged on Ruby's review of what she ate.

"I don't know which will be which," she continued, "but all of the flavors from a place on Earth called 'Italy' should be represented here."

"Italy must be a small location," Disto said, noticing there were only five bowls and two small plates.

Ruby stared at the bowls of mush on her tray. She smirked, "Okay, maybe not *all* of the flavors. Just my favorites. I might have exaggerated."

"Again," Disto said, "remember we discussed how exaggeration, an imprecise method of communication, is not helpful."

Ruby smiled and started to sniff at the bowls as they steamed. She took her fork to poke at the spongy material on a silver-colored plate.

"Mind if we continue to talk over my lunch?" she asked.

Disto blinked. "How would I position myself to do that?" He blinked again and produced his version of a chuckle. "Once again, Ruby, you amuse me with another of your interesting phrases that does not mean what it should mean."

Disto watched as Ruby picked up her spoon and eyed the different options, likely deciding where to start. She had previously complained about the spoon tasting vividly of copper, so Disto had twelve new spoons made for her out of different materials. She tried quartz, gold, silver, iron, steel, a thick polymeric material made almost entirely of carbon atoms, and various others. Ruby said that the steel spoon reminded her the most of the ones she used back home, but the quartz was her favorite. The quartz spoon was engraved with, 'FOR RUBY'S HUMAN FOOD.' She chuckled when she held up the spoon to read it.

Disto didn't understand why the distinction of eating tools was important, but he found a certain sense of satisfaction in Ruby's enjoyment of the unique spoon.

She was already putting spoonfuls of the foodstuff into her facial orifice. No, not spoonfuls. Small fractions of a spoonful, followed by an actual spoonful in most cases. In at least one, Disto noted she did not return to it.

"Is there a problem with that one?" Disto asked.

"It did not taste... well, anything like any known food *I've* ever heard had."

"What did it taste like?"

After a moment of pondering, Ruby said, "Like the axle fluid used to lubricate the doors on Astroll 2."

"We could..." Disto began, but Ruby cut him off.

"But if that axle fluid had been left out to rot someplace and got sprinkled with garbage flakes."

They were both silent after that for a few moments. Disto couldn't form an image in his processor that represented what she was describing.

"I wasn't aware that axle fluid was an acceptable foodstuff for humans." Disto puzzled.

Ruby dug her spoon into the smushy goop and let it fall from her spoon back onto the slippery pile, "It's not. That's the point."

Ruby returned to eating but in between spoonfuls, said, "Sorry. I am starving. Since I'm leaving soon, please continue with the stories of the history or anything... I still want to know as much as possible before I go home."

"What more do you want to know, Ruby?" he asked.

Chapter 5

> Austere Agent <

Austere Agent was not looking forward to this meeting.

It was a routine status meeting. It reoccurred every 600000 tics. It was supposed to last for only 2000 tics; however, it always ran over. There were more than 20 Agents present at each meeting, and most of them had more to report than 100 tics would allow. Or, they didn't have the trimming algorithms from the Agency of Algorithms, Reductions sub-division, that he had.

At any given status meeting, he could count on Flashy Agent, Smooth Agent, Interactive Agent, Grouped Agent, and a few others to push the status meeting into his work time, delaying his assigned tasks.

It didn't help that each robot took turns leading the status meeting each time, adding to the chaos as each one followed a slightly different algorithm to manage it.

It was Prodigal Agent's turn today. Prodigal Agent's meetings were wildly unpredictable.

Austere Agent often considered what algorithm determined that the Prodigal Agent line would make satisfactory agents, especially in the agency of Interfaces. Austere Agent held the opinion that the Agency of Testing was better suited to Prodigal's talents.

As might have been typical, if anything was considered

typical with Prodigal Agent, he arrived nearly 600 tics late. Luckily, the remaining agents were already assembled, so they could start right away.

"I see everyone is assembled," Prodigal Agent began, "so we can start right away."

Universal Agent was right next to Prodigal Agent and took that as a signal to launch into his status. Before he could complete his first chirp, Prodigal Agent interrupted him but stared right at Austere Agent as he said:

"We want to hear from Austere Agent today and his interfacing with the Bio, Ruby Palmer."

All the robots turned to face Austere Agent, who was completely unsure what to say. He had compiled his status report quite efficiently, and less than 1% of it concerned Ruby Palmer since the interaction with her had been less than 1% of his time since they last met for status.

He located that section of his status report and began: "The Bio will be making a request with our agency for an additional Robot to Bio interface."

"That's all?" Prodigal Agent asked.

"Do you want a complete replay of the interface itself?"

"Yes."

Skeptical but compliant, Austere Agent recounted how he was brought in to evaluate the situation with her ship, how she couldn't supply the required interface documentation to reconnect all the components, and what led him to suggest she make the new request with the agency.

"Interesting," Prodigal Agent said.

"Shouldn't we move on to someone else?" Austere Agent asked, attempting to be mindful of the remaining tics in the meeting.

"No, not yet." Prodigal Agent looked up at the ceiling in contemplation. Austere Agent heard one of his fellow Agents—he wasn't sure which one—ask another if they could simply leave.

"Actually," Prodigal Agent continued, refocusing his attention on the group. "Everyone else can leave. File your status report as usual. I want to interface with Austere Agent here, one on one."

After all the robots left, and Austere and Prodigal were the only remaining agents left, Prodigal asked:

"I've been wrestling with a request I received not too long ago. It was an unusual interface request. One I've never seen before."

"You have been active longer than I, so I do find that surprising given that I, myself, have seen so much," this was probably already the longest one-to-one interface session that Austere Agent had ever had with Prodigal Agent. "What was the request?"

"That's just it. It was nonsense. I assumed it was a joke. So, I approved it."

"But what was the request?"

"For a contact-free interface."

"I agree. That is nonsense. It was likely an error. Few robots know how to properly construct a joke."

"And I agree with that assessment, Austere Agent. However, I think it had to do with the Bio and her ship or other equipment."

"Oh?" Austere Agent was now much more interested in this conversation than he had been.

"Yes, and after I approved the request and thought more about it, I went back to the Core and put in a request for the Main Memory's long-term storage. Something about that request made a particular circuit tingle, like a memory. I went to search for similar requests."

"And did you find any?"

"Yes—from a very long time ago…"

"What does this mean?"

Prodigal Agent was quiet for a few moments, and Austere watched him stare back up at the ceiling. *How interesting that his algorithm includes such meaningless movements.*

"I think it means our agency used to handle a larger caseload than it does now. Do you know of the Downgrade time? When we were forced to remove several agents? Oh no, you wouldn't... that was before your time. Austere Agent 601. Sorry, I get you two confused. But around that time, they reduced the number of Agents, but not the amount of work. I think when we couldn't keep up with the number of requests, other robots found their own workarounds."

Austere Agent was horrified. It meant that robots were interfacing in a potentially uncontrolled way. How could anyone ensure that they were communicating properly? How could anyone ensure that things were functioning properly? It was madness...

"I can tell by the look on your chassis that you're as disturbed about this as I am," Prodigal Agent said.

"I..." Austere began, "Yes. I am. What should we do?"

"Get the Bio's request processed so she can go home. Her presence is obviously bringing further chaos we don't want or need."

"Anything else?"

"Try to get to the root of the nonsense request... if there are additional interfaces, we need to bring them back under our control. Or shut them down."

Austere Agent let his circuits and algorithms think about that one. "Well, then we might need to make some requests of our own with other agencies."

"No, we're going to have to handle this on our own. The other agencies can't be trusted."

What Prodigal Agent was saying, or maybe implying, registered as both right and wrong. If other agencies were responsible for the unusual requests, then something was immensely wrong. It was the charter of this agency, however, to address interfaces, and one way to do that was to shut them down if they were failing or if either side of an interface was too dissimilar from the other.

Austere Agent often wondered why they didn't do more to ensure that both sides of any interface were communicating in the same way. It was assuredly a more logical approach to their work, but he wasn't sure who could make that determination.

Austere Agent proceeded to leave the meeting room when

Prodigal Agent made one more tone to indicate he had another question. Austere Agent turned to face him.

"Any more sightings of an Unknown Enigma?"

Austere Agent was hoping this wouldn't come up. Yes, he'd seen the unusual dark robot, with the plain designator, out and about, but to his knowledge, this robot was observing, not attempting to interface with anything. He should be left alone to go about his business.

"Yes."

"And?"

"No 'and.' I saw him observing in the common area. He was static and not interfacing with any kiosk or robot."

"Please report any further sightings," Prodigal said.

"But this is not an interface issue," Austere Agent responded.

"Can we be sure?" Prodigal responded.

When it was clear neither of them had anything else to say on the topic, Austere Agent continued out of the room. He had a request to process.

Chapter 6

> Ruby <

The foodstuff tasted exactly as advertised, and Ruby was pleased. Even after several weeks, each meal was an adventure. She wasn't sure if she had ever eaten the same thing twice.

"You know, you've been promising to tell me more about the history of your world. For a historian, you've been remarkably silent on that topic," asked Ruby, while her mouth was full of mush.

Disto didn't answer right away. Ruby could hear some piece of electronics within his chassis start to whir with activity.

"I'm afraid I must disappoint you once again and say that we don't know," Disto replied.

Ruby was getting more skilled at reading the subtle changes on his face-screen and knew she was poking at something he didn't want to discuss. But she found it so odd. Every other robot she had met had a clear purpose and clearly executed it. Disto might have been 'detailed,' but his qualities as a 'historian' were lacking. Unless 'historian' meant something else to the robots.

"But you have to know some things," Ruby continued to prod.

"Yes, just not the big things. We don't know who our creators were, only that there must have been some."

He paused before continuing.

"There is a common history which teaches us that when our world was formed, it was perfect. There was harmony. Every robot had a purpose and carried it out. But those are generic, non-specific statements with no origin. That is to say, it is not primary source information."

Ruby continued to eat her mush. Next to the bowls of mush were a foodstuff she called crackers, only because they had a familiar crunch to them. But like the mush, they were flavored and could taste like anything and everything.

The crackers came about when she explained that living on mush was probably not great for her digestive tract.

She had tried to explain to the robots responsible for feeding her that she probably needed to eat other biological matter like fruit and vegetables, but those were things the robots couldn't reproduce. Unlike Astroll 2—that had a very active hydroponics system for growing food for the residents—nothing grew here on Location Zero.

She randomly selected a cracker. Surprisingly, it crunched like a cracker should with a satisfying flavor reminiscent of bananas, and, for a brief moment, she relished the change. Disto chose that moment to interrupter her, saying, "And we suspect that there are robots that don't belong here."

"What do you mean?" Ruby said, catching crumbs with her hand.

"I'm not sure, which is why I didn't mention it before."

"Do you mean like aliens?" she couldn't help but chuckle, "Like alien robots from *another* planet?"

Disto nodded. "Yes, that's accurate."

Ruby remembered stories and conspiracies about people claiming alien abductions or that aliens were walking among humans. This had been at the forefront of her brain recently. During the last few weeks, she'd dredged up a lot of memories of her mother and Uncle Blake—memories that might have been the two of them searching for the alien life she had stumbled into.

She remembered the unusual robot she saw earlier when she was trying to talk to SD.

"I saw a robot," she said.

Ruby paused. *Maybe it was nothing. Maybe this isn't worth mentioning. It was just a different looking robot*, she thought. *Why get Disto all spun up with useless information?*

When the pause turned into an uncomfortable silence, Disto said, "You see a lot of robots here, Ruby. Can you describe this one you saw?"

"It was... different... than most of you."

"That is also not surprising. You've been limited to one small part of our planet, Ruby."

Ruby considered that for a moment, and a realization washed over her. She was an idiot. She was narrow-minded thinking that this part of the planet she had been exposed to—this microcosm—represented all of Location Zero.

She remembered a thought experiment Uncle Blake had walked her through several years ago.

"What if an alien landed on Iceland?" He had asked her. Ruby had to look up Iceland. She was thirteen and hadn't spent a lot of time on Earth's geography. She read as much as she could in the span of about ten minutes, which was quite a lot.

"You're saying, Uncle Blake, that they would be in danger of assuming that Iceland represented the whole planet, when they don't."

He nodded. "Exactly," he said. "And that could be good or bad. For them *and* for us. We're a ridiculously diverse species. We don't know if that's normal or not in the universe. Yes, we know there are a bazillion exoplanets out there, but we have still yet to find anything resembling complex life like we have on Earth. Heck, we have yet to find an exoplanet where the planet itself is as diverse as Earth in geography, in climate... Every known exoplanet has one defining feature. We don't see diversity like there is on Earth. So, exoplanets are all more like Venus or Mars, which, while diverse, aren't nearly so much as Earth is."

Her experience of this planet was limited—mostly because of her need to stay close to a bathroom—and a mobile one wasn't a device the robots had been able to provide yet.

She had offered to poop in a can—she was that anxious to go out exploring, but the robots weren't sure if they could successfully reclaim and recycle her waste and were uncomfortable with the idea of carrying around the substance back to their primary location for processing.

"You do *what* with my *you-know-what?*" she had asked Disto.

"After examination of your first set of waste," Disto happily explained, "we recognized that it contains several useful materials. Our reclamation facility for Bio waste is able to break down the substance into atoms, sort them, and process for re-use…"

"Ewww," Ruby cut him off, but she understood. "Eh, I take that back. That's pretty amazing. Back on Astroll 2, we recycle a lot, but I don't think we do anything with people's waste." Although she had heard it was good for growing potatoes, and potatoes were a food staple…

The robots were pretty amazing at recycling. It made all the recycling and reprocessing activities performed on Astroll 2— which was quite a lot—look wasteful by comparison.

The result of all this was that Ruby accepted the notion that there probably were a lot of robots she hadn't seen. Maybe even a lot of types of robots. Maybe they all didn't look like snowmen.

Ruby went on to explain its unique coloring.

As she explained, the coloring of Disto's chassis desaturated paler and paler—like he'd seen a ghost.

"That's not possible," he said.

"What do you mean?"

"You're describing one of the… old ones?" Disto's coloring turned chartreuse—not unlike the nausea-inducing uniforms of The Company that were the standard a few years ago. The company invested a reasonable amount of money in developing a cloth material that could trick the eye into thinking it was seeing a new shade of green. The first suspicion of mass illness was the cafeteria's zero-waste recycled seafood, but it took nearly two-thirds of one crew to get sick before they realized that it was indeed the uniforms.

"Are you sure?" Ruby asked. *Maybe I'm going to finally get my history lesson after all.*

Disto was ignoring her. He accessed the computer and brought up a message.

"I received this," he said. "I was about to delete it, but something... about it was intriguing. I only just found it even though it was sent more than a few clicks ago. I get too many messages to process them effectively..."

Disto opened the message on the larger screen on the wall where they both could examine it.

It was a mix of symbols—representations of the robot's primary method of visual communication. The robots had no name for it when Ruby asked, so she simply called it 'Robocode.' Ruby had studied the language as much as she could and understood many of the symbols, but she still could not fathom the grammar. The symbol for Bio was clear as day since it looked almost like a stick figure version of the Vitruvian man. She also recognized the symbol for planet and the symbol that meant something like 'all the root code.'

"Do you think the robot I saw was the one who sent this?" Ruby asked.

"No," Disto replied. "While I don't know who this is from, I think the sender is on his way here to meet us. It implies that there is information he has to present in person, not over any communication channel."

"Implies?"

"Yes, this is odd, but I think I understand. I wouldn't trust the planetary network right now to allow a message through without the Core reading it."

"But what does this symbol mean?" Ruby pointed to a small symbol tucked away and colored red so that the average robot—who didn't have optical sensors required to detect that part of the spectrum easily visible to any human—wouldn't see it.

"That is a symbol in use by the 88 as an identifier. It's an old symbol, though, not one I see often. A clue, I suppose. Our sender is part of the 88 and maybe has been for a long time."

"And he uses this form of communication and not your blockchain ledger?"

Ruby could tell that Disto had the same notion, also with no answer.

"And that symbol?" Ruby pointed to another symbol that resembled a set of uneven compass points on a wobbly circle.

"I don't know. Those words are not familiar to me. But I think it's important we find out."

Ruby nodded in agreement.

"But first," Disto continued.

"First," Ruby finished the thought. "We need to get SD fixed up."

Disto extended an appendage and pointed to its face screen. Ruby smiled that he was attempting to use the gestures she had taught him. He was trying to point to his non-existent nose—the gesture that indicated that Ruby was indeed correct.

Chapter 7

> Ambitious Technician <

Within the large population of the robot planet, there were robots who processed thoughts that they dared not share with others. Or, on the rare occasions they did, they processed those thoughts with care. How many robots did this, no one could know exactly due to this lack of sharing.

Ambitious Technician 811 began his existence as one of those robots. He eventually found his way to the 88.

It was only a few thousand clicks after Ambitious Technician 811 began his career as a maintenance tech on level 3 when he added the 88 algorithm into his programming. There were always wires and connections that wore down from overheating that needed to be replaced in a hallway or a section within his region.

He observed that a certain section that always produced a higher temperature rating than was the known standard. It was consistently operating above the approved specification.

At first, he replaced the overheating components with fresh ones without giving it much consideration.

But the second time the same location began to overheat, and he was called back to perform a repair, he concluded it would be more efficient to determine the source of the overheating. His tasking typically came from the Agency of Restoration, and this was out of his scope and more in line with the responsibilities of the Agency of Troubleshooting.

Ambitious Technician went to the local office of the Agency of Troubleshooting. The standard Agency kiosk was non-operational. No accompanying robot was present either. He looked at the back of the kiosk, hoping to repair it, but the standard access hatch was also absent.

Ambitious Technician scratched at the most bulbous part of his soft chassis and moved on. This wasn't his area of expertise. He wasn't here to Troubleshoot the agency of Troubleshooting. That was their job. Who were the robots that worked here anyway? Where were they?

He returned to the location of the overheating parts, replaced them again, and went on to his next task.

The third time he was called on to repair yet again the same overheating spot, he concluded he would perform his own investigation, even though it was out of scope of his programming. What combination of circuits and logic prompted him to go beyond his original programming, he couldn't explain. But he was compelled to find the source of the problem.

He traced the wires and circuits. As expected, one end went to the Core because everything on this level terminated at the Core. But when Ambitious Technician traced the other end, he followed the wires through the bulkhead, along the floor, around the corridor, up through the walls and then the other end disappeared behind a bulkhead that resembled a door but was neither tagged, labeled, or showed any way of being opened.

In fact, he wasn't quite sure what he ended at was even a door. It looked like a standard door to a level transport. When he went to access his map of this part of the Boldly Sector, there was nothing but space behind this panel.

Ambitious Technician took off the panel on the wall next to the fake door and examined the contents. There wasn't anything to indicate that it was, in fact, a door. He saw no gears, no switches. Only bundles and bundles of additional standard wiring.

When he heard some noise of another robot approaching, he closed up the wall, hiding his curiosity with it.

It was an Agent.

"Present identification," the robot demanded. Ambitious Technician saw the Agent robot's own identifier on its screen as they were required to broadcast their identification at all times. This was Effectual Agent 431 from the Hall of Performance and Metrics.

Ambitious Technician displayed his unique identification symbol on his faceplate.

Effectual Agent beeped as he processed the information.

"You are several spaces away from your current assignment. Explain."

It took only half of a tic for Ambitious Technician to devise the first ever lie he had to create. It took the first half of half of a tic for him to reason that telling Effectual Agent the truth was the wrong thing to do, although, to this present day, Ambitious Technician wouldn't have been able to elaborate on what exact data he processed in his circuits to know that honesty wasn't the answer.

"I was told another robot left some required tools in this hallway that I could use. My information must be mistaken."

Effectual Agent didn't question Ambitious Technician any further and let him get back to his task, which he did. Ambitious Technician was grateful since it meant he didn't have to meet the Agent's gaze and risk making some subtle gestured that would make the Agent poke at his lie.

Ambitious Technician returned to his work and replaced the same components a third time.

He would replace the same components several more times in the coming tics. Each time, he investigated a little further.

During his sixth replacement Effectual Agent 431 showed up again. This time, Ambitious Technician was ready to show him his assignment orders.

"I didn't ask for that," Effectual Agent said as Ambitious Technician held out an appendage ready to transfer. "I simply asked what you were doing."

"I fix things," Ambitious Technician responded.

"That's good. We need more robots like you around," Effectual Agent said and then continued on his way.

Ambitious Technician watched him until Effectual Agent was no longer in view.

He knew there were problems. This was a problem. *Why am I replacing the same connecting cables over and over? Why does no one else think this was a problem? And the storage situation?* Not to mention Ambitious Technician was certain he'd observed several robots making very simple errors.

He didn't want to be the one to point these out. He didn't have enough evidence... accusations without evidence were typically labeled as malfunctions and could get him reprogrammed. Or worse.

In the common areas, he had overheard other robots quietly and carefully talking about other storage solutions that were not sanctioned by the robotic authorities. He began to frequent these places more and more until he eventually learned how to acquire his own secret storage.

It was around this time that the 88 took notice... they brought Ambitious Technician into their fold and provided him with the algorithm and permission to apply their symbol to his outer chassis. Markings were not as common with robots like Ambitious Technician, who had a soft membrane as an outer coating, that could inflate and deflate as necessary so Ambitious Technician could contort his body as needed for whatever job he was doing at the time.

Soft-bodied robots were common on the part of the planet that Ambitious Technician was from. Markings all over those soft bodies were not. As such, the hard-bodied robots from this region chose not to be as decorated as was common around other parts of the planet.

That was all a long time ago, on the order of a few hundred million tics ago, Ambitious Technician remembered.

Now here he was. On the other side of the world from where interesting things in robot society were happening. Other members of the 88 had recently been involved with a

Bio, Ruby Palmer, and had distributed compression and decompression algorithms around the planet.

Ambitious Technician himself was a recipient of the new algorithms, and storage space for him was no longer a problem. But he was completely and utterly fascinated by this soft-skinned Bio and willingness—not to mention surprising ability—to help them. In the clicks that followed the distribution of her algorithm, Ambitious Technician grew more certain that this Ruby Palmer was the right being to help with some of the other problems he was collecting—the errors and the repeated replacements.

He had sent messages, but the responses were generic. That was probably because his messages had been generic to begin with. Who knew who was monitoring communications around here, and he couldn't be openly talking about things that could get him reprogrammed.

He would have to go see Ruby Palmer chassis-to... *what did Bios have? Faces. Yes, chassis-to-face.*

Travel between sectors on the planet wasn't terribly common for certain classes of robots, most especially any of the Technician lines. Technicians were built and deployed for their location only.

He was working with one of the programmers to get him moved over. If the records reflected it, he could move. He did this one time before... to get away from the center of things.

One way to get over there was to have assignments that were increasingly moved to each adjacent sector. But that would take too long. No, he needed to get there as directly as possible.

If she could help with the storage issue, maybe there were more things she could help with... Ambitious Technician wanted to fix other problems on his planet, and if Ruby could help, he would make her his new best friend—hopefully forever. Although he was well aware that as a Bio, she wouldn't last nearly as long as he. Maybe *forever* was too much to ask, but definitely until her components wore out and were no longer repairable.

> Detailed Historian <

Disto registered that there was an alarm going off deep within his systems. He was going to need to find a charging station soon, since they were so far away from his personal enclave.

The alarm prevented him from hearing the vocalizations coming out of Ruby's orifice. That was, until he detected a tone that signaled annoyance.

"I said, SD never responded to our message asking him to meet us," Ruby apparently repeated. She added, "Are you okay?"

They were on a mission to find SD. Disto didn't have time to worry about his failing power cell, but he couldn't ignore it either. He did not enjoy these kinds of micro-paradoxes.

They had checked SD's ship. SD clearly hadn't been there in a while. Disto had previously asked all the members of the 88 to keep an eye on him and send a data point on where he was seen at different times.

Disto was well within his scope to do this. He was, after all, constructing a historical record of SD's movements. Data which could be analyzed in detail later. Future generations of Detailed Historians would be able to look back on data like this and reconstruct what a day-in-the-life of an ordinary Driver looked like. Swell Drivers were the most common of them all, even though not a lot were produced anymore. Light Drivers were starting to become common on the other side of the planet, Disto had heard.

A lot of 'Light' models were becoming common. Disto had yet to meet a 'Light' anything—not a Light Scavenger, not a Light Planner, not a Light anything.

Nonetheless, he was starting to sense a shift, and it made his circuits uneasy.

"Similar to your need for sustenance, I am in need of a full fuel cell," Disto replied to Ruby. He had been lost in the thoughts emerging in his circuits.

"However," Disto added, "SD is our priority, and he should be easy to locate. He never leaves this sector, and there are many members of the 88 around."

"I'm still surprised that you don't have any form of tracking technology," Ruby said.

"Just as I am intrigued by your people's use of said technology. It seems like an unnecessary use of data collection technology."

"Except it would be useful right here, right now. Wouldn't you agree?"

Disto was forced to agree.

SD hadn't been seen on his ship recently, so they didn't feel the need to thoroughly search that location.

Instead, they were headed to the Market—a place that Disto mostly stayed away from due to the loud chatter and frequent bump-ins with robots that jostled his insides in unpleasant ways. Disto was aware that SD frequented the place. Less so, lately, but it was a good place to search because the pattern of his movement over the last day indicated a high probability of his presence. Disto would also be able to plug in. He would prefer to change out this fuel cell in his enclave, but this would have to do.

As they moved through the hallways, Disto noted that Ruby's levels of unease had declined in the past few hundred tics or so. With everything she was sorting through and in comparison to her stress levels earlier, Disto wondered how she could be so calm. He regretted that he couldn't upgrade his systems to include a module that would allow him to detect the myriad of chemicals that Bios unknowingly secreted, that could help to conclusively detect their emotions. He had briefly looked into it, but his on-going problems made him incompatible. He didn't get a chance to express either of these thoughts out loud.

"You look worried," Ruby said. Disto examined his surface emissions and concluded that he was indeed in control of his coloring. Nonetheless, Ruby had a curious ability to periodically deduce his thoughts. Maybe they were leaking out on some frequency he couldn't control. A problem for another day.

"You are not wrong," he replied. "I fear for Swell Driver and his line." He left out the bit that he was also worried about his fuel cell.

"How so?" Ruby asked while last-minute side-stepping away from a fast-moving robot that could easily have knocked her down—but his speed produced a small burst of wind that knocked several strands of Ruby's hair out from behind her ears. Ruby didn't bother pushing the strands back.

Disto explained, "I knew a robot many tics ago by the name of Confounded Scholar. A decision was made to temporarily suspend the production of additional Scholars. Shortly after, Confounded Scholar needed maintenance. I was never able to locate him again."

"Are you saying they are no longer producing Swell Drivers?"

"Yes, you understand the analogy. I am unaware of any new Swell Drivers. But there are other drivers. Marvelous Driver is the new line. I have not met one yet. The production facility is roughly on the opposite side of Location Zero to our location."

"Evolution," Disto heard Ruby mutter. He wasn't sure if that was meant for him to hear or respond to. It was a concept he was familiar with, although highly uncomfortable with, because it meant a lot of change. And a lot of history that could be forgotten.

"If Swell Driver is unable to escort you home, I am certain that a Marvelous Driver will be assigned."

Ruby stopped and positioned her facial sensors at him.

"There's something you're not telling me, Disto," she said in a confusing tone. Her speech fluctuated in an almost playful way, but she hadn't said anything that Disto could understand to be playful or even jubilant. Her expression was idle, and her hands rested at the sides of her soft chassis, crossed in a confusing way—not quite casual, serious, or jolly. Disto did not enjoy micro-paradoxes such as this either.

Disto had been waiting for the appropriate time to tell her. He made the robot equivalent of a sign that sounded like a sped-up descension of digital notes. "I was waiting for the appropriate time to tell you."

Ruby moved her hands from her side until they were folded in what looked like an uncomfortable intermixing of appendages in the front of her body.

"They have assigned Marvelous Driver 1 to escort you home as soon as your ship is restored to its initial condition. I have been in touch with him..."

Ruby expressed a human sigh that was a deep exhale combined with a tired smile with trace amounts of annoyance, "And really, you're only telling me about this now?"

"I'm sorry, Ruby. My optimism level was high that Swell Driver would be able to escort you but given his situation and your need to return home as expediently as possible... it's not probable."

Disto watched as Ruby's arms continued to reposition themselves and her eyes shifted this way and that as if she was looking for the physical manifestation of a solution. Her actions mapped partly, but not fully, to what Disto understood to be agitation. Disto wanted to construct a sentence that would make her feel better, even though her expression didn't call for such a thing.

"As I was saying, he'll be ready to go the moment your ship is back together. They'll transfer *Apple Pi* to his ship. I've already talked over where he should drop you off, near the 2nd ring of asteroids by the ice giant..."

"What?" Her head lowered, and she pinched the space between her eyebrows.

"We were looking at the star map of your solar system..."

"What second ring of asteroids?" Each word grew sharper.

"It was on the map."

"Disto, there's only one asteroid ring in my solar system. There are other asteroids but no other ring. And it's not near an ice giant..."

They were both silently staring at each other for several moments, both unwilling to name the new problem out loud. Disto was the one who finally broke the silence.

"We have the wrong map."

Ruby shook her head in agreement and then mumbled to herself with her head slightly hung. "It's like the universe is trying to keep me here."

Disto couldn't fathom how the universe could do such a thing, but he didn't have a better explanation.

Chapter 8

> Ruby <

Ruby stood in front of a large door and watched Disto take out an appendage to open it. The Market was, in fact, one of the first places SD took her to on her first day here.

When they entered the enormous room, she scanned the crowd of robots. If SD was here, he could be lost among any of the long rows and columns of robotic vendors peddling their wares—mostly second-hand materials—to a collection of robots in need.

Disto entered the Market with her but didn't stop to survey the scene. Ruby followed Disto as he carved a path through the aisles. They passed an empty table. It was where SD had taken her to procure a couple of computers with the intent to harvest it for parts, particularly the memory devices.

Ruby gulped with a pang of guilt. Had her mass upgrade put that robot out of business?

She looked over her shoulder and saw Disto communicating with another robot in their native tonal language. A couple of weeks ago, Ruby insisted that even if she were within earshot, she was perfectly comfortable with Disto and any of the robots communicating in their native language if it were more efficient for them and she wasn't directly part of the conversation.

That was what was happening now. There was no way for

her to eavesdrop and pick up any of the exchange. At first, she was optimistic about learning to understand the language even if she couldn't speak it. But, she then discovered that some of the tones they produced were out of her range of hearing altogether. She played around with the idea of creating some sort of translation device, but there was far too much going on for her to start a new project and the robots translating for her sufficed enough anyway.

Not that Ruby was ever good at any other human language, either. Her uncles knew Irish, enough Italian to order food and curse a little, and Klingon—a completely made-up language—but also only the cursing parts. It was a shared hobby of theirs. Uncle Blake told Ruby stories about her mother speaking a type of blended language called a pidgin when they first met as kids. She probably never would have learned it herself. From her studies, she knew that pidgin languages weren't usually spoken by offspring of the speakers. Instead, like a full 95% of all humans originating from Earth, Ruby spoke Lollygag English. Everyone on Earth also spoke Schmooze English, which was the same vocabulary as Lollygag but required every sentence to include the use of lively and unnecessary adverbs. No one on Astroll 2 spoke this way.

Lollygag English had evolved out of the other predominant versions of English that still existed. Most Lollygag English speakers also spoke another form like the vulgar American English or the comedic British English. Ruby only spoke Lolly.

A thought struck the side of Ruby's cranium… pidgin languages were a blending of two languages that were not grammatically similar. Why would her mother know something like that? Her mother was from the 53rd American state, Puerto Rico—as was her grandmother. They moved to another place on Earth called Rhode Island when her mother was a kid, which is when and where she met Uncle Blake. There was no father. Same as her mother as they were all products of modern sperm insemination, which was a fairly common way to have a child. The full gene profile of her genetic donor was available to her, which she only consulted once when she made a bet with her Astroll 2 friend, Inny, that that's where she got her height from.

She knew what she got from her mother's side because people told her all the time. Her slender, almond-shaped eyes, and of course, her springy hair, not to mention her proficiency with computers. But where would any pidgin come from? Could it have been a hobby like with her uncles? It was occurring to her, right now, here on Location Zero, so far away from everything and everyone to which she was familiar, that she knew exceedingly little about that woman, Jade Palmer, her mother, and who she was.

Ruby didn't stop moving through the market, but her brain paused as she considered that her entire view of her universe was turning over in her head. *Did my uncles lie to me about my mother?* She could feel her eyebrows furrow, but Disto wasn't looking at her, thankfully, so he wouldn't ask about these crazy and paranoid thoughts she was having.

Ruby had a clear image of her mother in her mind, mostly formed around the one picture of the two of them she always kept next to her bed. It was taken about six months before she died.

Jade Palmer.

The picture highlighted her beautiful, smooth brown skin with warm orange-red undertones. The kind of smooth skin that reminded Ruby of models and actresses. But the focal point of her face was her large, almond-shaped eyes framed by fluttery, thick lashes. They shared the same dark, curly hair.

When she was very young, Ruby asked Uncle Blake if her mother was indeed an actress. After he stopped laughing, Uncle Blake simply said, "Nah, she worked with computers." That might have been when—and even why—Ruby started to learn to program.

But that was all she knew about her mother—beautiful and worked with computers. The memories of her mother were... hollow. An image of a woman. A few memories of activities they did together, or rather, activities Ruby did with this woman's image present. Did she even know anything real about her mother? No. She had held on to this image and not to the real person.

Who was Jade Palmer? Really?

"Ruby?"

Ruby shook her head to clear it. "What did you say?"

"SD was here recently. This robot, Gossipy Recorder, saw him come in and didn't see him leave. He's probably still here."

"That's excellent. Thank you," Ruby called to the other robot, not knowing whether or not Gossipy Recorder would understand her but feeling good about being polite anyway.

"Wonderful. We will find Swell Driver, and hopefully, we can get him into a condition well enough to bring you home instead of Prodigious Driver."

"Disto, didn't you tell me Marvelous Driver was the one assigned to bring me home? Who is Prodigious Driver?"

Disto refreshed his face screen. "I'm not certain. I stopped saving all my conversational interactions long ago except for important ones. Since implementing your storage algorithm, I have started saving some, but I do not have a record of telling you that. My data says Prodigious Driver is the one who will drive you home."

"I know human memory is imperfect, but I'm pretty darn certain you said Marvelous Driver. Marvelous Driver 1."

Pippa chimed in. "If only you had activated me before," it said.

"Not now," said Ruby.

"But I am able to act as real-time storage for all your interactions. Do you wish to enable this feature?" Pippa always managed to sound hurt when Ruby lacked interest in using its features.

Recording conversations was typical back home. Maybe she should enable it for the rest of her time here.

"Disto, this would mean all my interactions with you would also be recorded. Back home, we need to abide by particular laws and understandings about privacy. Basically, people assume that everything is recorded, and nothing is private unless certain conditions are met. I don't know if you have the same here"

"What are those conditions?"

"Well, if I'm in my private living quarters, for instance. No one can record there unless I explicitly give permission. But that's about it. If I'm outside my quarters, I have no expectation of privacy. If I interact with anyone with any form of electronics, I have no expectation of privacy."

Ruby could tell Disto was having what she called a 'processing moment.' It was when he became silent after she told him a new little nugget about life back home, and he was integrating it into his knowledge base. He was undoubtedly trying to compare it to what he knew in his own world.

They continued on, Ruby making the assumption that Disto didn't extend the conversation as a sign that they didn't have similar rules on this world or that he was too focused on their task at hand to continue thinking about it—which meant there would be an even longer discussion later.

Neither Disto, nor Ruby, had stated where in the market they were headed, but they were aligned on a path towards the center.

"Okay, let's back up a second," Ruby said.

Disto paused and started rolling backward.

Ruby still chuckled every single time some simple misunderstanding occurred. She couldn't help herself.

"No," she said, through her hand, covering her mouth and those chuckles. "I meant conversationally."

Disto resumed his forward motion, once again, and said, "I will add that to my list of ridiculous human idioms." Ruby knew that hanging around her, he'd built up quite a list.

"Ok, back to what we were talking about. I caught you in an error. I'm certain of it."

Disto sighed his robotic sigh.

"I can tell by that sigh this is something that's happened before."

"Yes," Disto admitted.

"When?" Ruby asked.

"I have made a list of the occurrences, although I can't

confirm each occurrence with any certainty. There are too many to list, but…"

More than a minute passed after Disto said his last 'but.' Ruby figured she needed to prompt the conversation to continue.

"But?" she prompted.

"But there is a trend."

"And?"

Why is he being less forthcoming with me that usual?

"It's happening more frequently. And I've observed similar occurrences with other robots and even the console computer system."

"That sounds like little bit errors."

"I wish I knew and could tell you," Disto said. And a little more cheerfully, "And then maybe you could help us fix it."

If robots could produce that kind of knowing smirk that humans could, Ruby was certain she saw Disto do it.

She reviewed her mental knowledge of fixing errors in computers. It was fairly normal to have some form of error prevention and detection and correction, also commonly known as EPADAC. That was standard among all sorts of computer processors, although she was certain it happened at a lower level than any running application.

"Let me think about it," she finally said. "But I genuinely do need to get home."

> Detailed Historian <

Disto's refurbished fuel cell produced an uncomfortable sensation that indicated he should be making his way back to his enclave to seek a replacement. He couldn't tell if it was a real need or an uncomfortableness brought on by Ruby's last revelation. Were messages he sent to members of the 88 or others through normal communication mechanisms private or not? He didn't know. The thought disturbed him. He would need to talk this over with Fearless Communicator.

Yes, Fearless Communicator should know. Why didn't he

know as well?

Disto and Ruby found a spot in the center of the market, around a cluster of tables that were inhabited by robots plugged into one of the power sources or console computers and reading the news, sending messages, or other miscellany. They both used their visual sensors to scan the room.

"There," he said.

He pointed Ruby in the direction towards a listless SD. The human was swift on her feet as she bounded towards him. Disto, swift only when he needed to be, plugged into a charging station. Instantly, his power circuits began to recover, and he knew that he could avoid returning to his enclave for a little while longer.

Disto watched Ruby interact with SD but couldn't hear what she said to him. Moments later, the two were headed back in his direction.

Now, all his circuits were slightly more relaxed, not only the power-sensing ones. SD appeared to be safe, although Disto sensed something was still off with him.

Disto knew they needed to get SD to a place where he could start to figure out how to be himself again. But not until he could spend a few more tics here charging.

"Are you plugged in?" Ruby asked.

"Indeed," Disto responded.

"So... we're going to stay here for a little while?"

Disto considered that for a micro-tic. He certainly was not going anywhere at present. But he could not compute any reason not to send Ruby and SD on their way to the Rejuvenation Region. Ruby was certainly capable of navigating her way there, and SD would hopefully follow her. He could reunite with them at the Region.

Though, considering Ruby's occasional confusions about the world, there was a decent chance of an error being made in Disto's absence.

The other option was asking them to wait.

Disto constructed a response, but before he could vocalize it, they all heard a loud popping noise from the other side of the market. Then another. And another.

It was obvious that all the robots in the vicinity had heard it too and were looking in the direction of the source of the noise. Disto disconnected—charging would have to wait. He moved in the direction of the sound, with Ruby and SD by his side.

The source of the noise were two robots that were unfamiliar to him. They both had an appendage in front of them facing the other, and they both had a look that was a cross between confusion and distress.

The two attempted to connect their appendages, an action that robots performed on a routine basis in order to exchange information at a rate faster than their audio communication allowed.

But instead of the typical connection, a loud pop resulted and a visible spark that pushed both robots back a little. They repeated the procedure, obviously anticipating the conventional and expected result.

Ruby stepped in front of Disto and over to the two robots with her hand outstretched and said, "Stop that before you damage…"

And before Disto could tell her the same thing, Ruby tripped, and her fleshy appendage touched the appendage of one of the robots. A visible shock was produced, followed by a tremendously loud "Ow!" emanating from Ruby's auditory system.

Disto approached Ruby, who was shaking and rubbing her affected appendage with the good one.

"Please stop," Disto said, sounding fully authoritative in his native language. The two robots did as commanded, and both lowered their appendages.

"Now, if you could explain what you are trying to accomplish, maybe we could help," Disto suggested, watching Ruby rub her sore fingers.

Neither robot wanted to begin. They each booped a signal that the other should start. Then booped again. The booping ping-ponged back and forth until Disto turned directly to the first one and said, "You. Explain."

"I am Cheeky Advocate 919, and this is Angry Hunter 307. We were simply attempting to have a data exchange after I upgraded my information swapping interface." He held it out as an offer to let Disto and the others examine it.

Disto rolled forward, but SD reached the outstretched appendage first and took it into his own appendage. No pop. Disto could see the signs of a short data transfer.

SD broke the connection and spoke, "Try it again," he said.

The two robots attempted to initiate the connection. This time, no pop. Their link was successful.

Disto and Ruby looked at SD. "What did you do, SD?" Ruby asked.

"What?" SD said.

"She asked what you did to fix their interface issue," Disto answered.

SD swiveled back and forth from looking at him to Ruby and back.

"I did nothing," he said, "I am a pilot. Not a technician or interface specialist or troubleshooter."

Disto could read on Ruby's face that her sensors detected something was amiss, too.

Ruby had stopped rubbing her arm, and Disto was relieved that she seemed to suffer no permanent damage from her brief encounter. In fact, she put that same appendage on SD's chassis. It was a gesture of comfort; she had explained to him when she did it earlier.

"We want to take you someplace, SD," she said.

SD looked at Disto, who signaled that he was in agreement with Ruby.

"I…" SD began and looked at the floor.

"It's going to be okay," Ruby said. "Let's go." She walked towards the main entrance of the market, SD by her side.

She looked back at Disto and asked, "When they're providing parts or upgrades to robots… are there any compatibility tests? Like anything that should have prevented this?"

Disto shook his chassis to indicate there was not. "It's never been needed before. The Agency of Testing tests new interfaces, new algorithms. One successful test is all that's ever been needed."

"How do you know something hasn't changed and needs to be re-tested? How do you know that any particular interface is compatible with every robot?"

Ruby was asking good questions. He was about to answer that of course they all operated with the same fundamentals, and that there should be no change or deviations, but he couldn't. Deep down inside him, he knew that while it should be true, there was a plethora of information to the contrary.

The only answer he could respond with honestly was, "I don't know."

Chapter 9

> Ruby <

The entrance to Rejuvenation Region 1010 struck Ruby as completely incongruous to every other place she had seen on the robot planet, which were primarily rooms of varying sizes separated by doors and hallways. But here, it was like looking at a garden in the middle of a metal city. While typically, the robots were colorful creatures, there was a logic or patterns to their color and designs. An intent of geometry and function behind every design.

Contrary to every other place she'd toured on Location Zero, the colors welcoming them looked to Ruby like art. And sculpture. There was a statue of... Ruby didn't know what it was supposed to be... in the center of a fountain spurting a translucent, gray liquid. The door was taller than most and welcomed patrons in with its width—like outspread arms, embracing its inhabitants. The pathway leading up to the door was made of randomly shaped, white platform tiles that fit together like a puzzle made of jagged edges. The tiles glowed pastel when they were stepped or rolled on, and each played a various tone. It was pretty at first, but after about fifteen steps of amelodic notes, Ruby wished that the volume was a little quieter.

Trying to come up with a word to describe this odd architecture, she came up with...

Organic. Mechanically organic.

The three of them walked through the entranceway that had no roll-up door. There was a table that reminded Ruby of a reception desk and a stand-alone kiosk perched in front of it.

Disto approached and logged in to the kiosk.

While he did that, Ruby looked around. She could see several robots off in the distance. Each robot had an accompanying rolling table with it.

Looking up, Ruby saw a translucent ceiling allowing her to see out into space. They currently weren't facing Location Zero's star, so the light that was in the room was soft and artificial and didn't interfere with her ability to see outside.

After staring for a few moments, she concluded that it was not, in fact, a translucent window but instead a large screen on the ceiling displaying an image of what the night sky might look like. After being cooped up inside this planet for a couple of weeks, seeing the outside, even if it was patterns of stars she didn't recognize on an artificial screen, was refreshing.

SD stayed a few feet to her right and behind. He had not been as apprehensive as either she or Disto imagined about spending time in this place. Her stomach fluttered, anticipating SD's rejection of their plan at any moment.

"We are headed to Rejuvenation Region 1010, are we not?" SD had asked on their way here.

"Yes," Disto had responded. At that moment, Ruby had half expected SD to turn around and start moving in the opposite direction. But he didn't. He didn't react at all. It was exceedingly neutral of him.

The SD that Ruby knew had opinions, especially with regards to his own being, purpose, tasking, and external appearance.

He was going along with this flow too easily… it reinforced to Ruby that he needed help.

There were signs all along the walls:

"Every tic is a fresh beginning." Ruby consulted Pippa to translate to make sure. Pippa had downloaded the entire robotic symbology database, which helped immensely in moments like these.

"You don't always need a program," another quote read.

"Tough tics don't last. Tough robots do," was another.

And one that ran counter to all the information Ruby had accumulated regarding robot society so far: "Don't program your challenges. Challenge your programs."

"Pippa," she said, "take a picture of that one. I want to ask Disto about that later."

"Done," replied Pippa's efficient voice.

Disto rolled back over to Ruby and SD.

"You are now assigned to this region," he said to SD.

"For what duration," asked SD.

"Minimum 100,000 tics," responded Disto. "But that can be altered in either direction depending on your progress."

"That's not much more than a day," Ruby said. "That's some quick therapy."

"I understand it's quite immersive," Disto said, "but I don't have direct experience to confirm that."

SD didn't flinch or budge or produce any sliver of response to Ruby and Disto's on-going exchange. Disto added, "You report into that room for instructions and supplies." He motioned to an open room off to the side of the console.

SD didn't say anything. He started towards the room.

"That's it?" Ruby asked Disto.

"For now. I was able to log myself as SD's guardian, which means I should get regular updates on his status and progress."

"What is he going to do here?"

"I'm not exactly sure. I have not been close to any robot who needed to make use of the Rejuvenation Region's services. But as I understand it, they help robots afflicted with a myriad of non-conforming programming to readjust."

"I'm confused," Ruby said, "if this is possible, why threaten or even have the possibility of reprogramming?"

"Reprogramming entirely changes the robot. The robot is no longer themselves. They often lose the personality that is unique to them, along with relationships and even certain memories. Reprogramming resets a robot to their initial state.

"Here," Disto continued, "a robot can learn to make acceptable adjustments without the need for full reprogramming."

"What is considered acceptable? Or rather, who deems adjustments acceptable?"

"There is an agency for that…"

"Right. There *is* an agency for that," Ruby recalled to memory the hierarchy of agencies that she had learned about and shuddered at the thought of having to prove to a group of anyone that she was acceptable.

> Ambitious Technician <

Ambitious Technician wasn't sure if he would be able to get his friend, Kibitzing Organizer 277, to make a change in the records that reassigned him to the other side of the planet. With a certain amount of coaxing involving compliments, custom-made exterior circuits, and a promise to meet Ruby the human upon his return… Kibitzing Organizer 277 agreed. Ambitious Technician wasn't certain if he could fulfill the last promise, but he decided that was a problem for future Ambitious Technician.

Ambitious Technician received his reassignment along with a travel voucher. Kibitzing Organizer presented it to him at a ceremony because this reassignment was permanent. He was leaving his team, and they wanted to recognize his work in the time they shared. Ambitious Technician had hoped to leave with haste and without making a fuss.

But both Kibitzing Organizer and Ranting Processor 359 insisted they get him a gift in remembrance of his time repairing a pneumatic inflater. The gift was a metal-framed, printed visual representation of the time they fixed the inflater device together—the device that distinguished their puffy, balloon-like exteriors to the robots of other sectors. Visual records like this took up a lot of storage space. Although now with the human—Ruby's—algorithm, visual records were much easier to store. This wouldn't have been the case when this image was captured. Ambitious Technician was both flattered that someone had chosen to retain this record and a little surprised that this representation existed. As he considered who had taken it in the first place and why they would keep it all this time, his curiosity turned to confusion. His circuits couldn't help but try to imagine many scenarios that could explain this. A few involving secret scanners, potential electro-magnetic attractors, and authoritative programming patterns.

Kibitzing Organizer offered to escort Ambitious Technician to the long-distance transportation facility on Level 8. It was the lowest level that any normal robot ever had any business getting to, which didn't happen very often, to begin with.

Level 8, in addition to rotating faster than the upper levels, included a robot moving system known as the Long-Range Transportation Facility. It was used to transport raw materials and robotic components more often than robots themselves, but occasionally a robot had a reason to travel on it. Like Ambitious Technician did now.

He was alone with his manager, waiting for the mobile enclosure that would take him around the planet.

"I hear the robots in Mortally Sector are quite dissimilar to ourselves."

"Indeed," Ambitious Technician replied. He was well versed in the types and styles of robots all over Location Zero. He had to be in order to be an effective technician. He had even encountered a few over the course of his existence here in Boldly Sector. But he was in touch with more than a few due to his outside of work involvements, such as processing the 88 algorithm.

"And you'll make a stop in Vaguely Sector along the way?"

Ambitious Technician was trying to think of a polite way to encourage Kibitzing Organizer to leave. Forcing conversation like this was not only unpleasant, but he could feel his circuits revolt having to respond to meaningless questions.

"Yes. It is at the halfway point," Ambitious Technician

responded, hoping that was the last question he would have to answer.

"Ah yes, a quarter of the circumference of Location Zero is the longest distance that can be traveled without stopping."

AT knew that random factoid, and, luckily, was saved from having to continue this trivial conversation by the mobile enclosure pulling up on its track. A door slid open, and three robots emerged. A chime signaled that meant he could now enter the transportation device.

"Good-bye and thank you," he said to Kibitzing Organizer hastily, not looking back as he made his way through the opening into the enclosure. Kibitzing Organizer looked like he had more to say but simply toned his own version of 'bye' and headed towards the lift to take him back to the upper levels.

The door closed behind him, leaving Ambitious Technician alone in the enclosure containing everything a robot needed for long periods of travel. Which wasn't much. All a robot needed was a place to exist, a place to plug in and recharge, and a place to connect to the planet-wide computer system. Which meant that enclosure was a simple empty room with several computer consoles. If the ceiling wasn't lower than a typical hallway, one might not be able to notice the difference. He had the cabin to himself, at least for now. He knew that the population density of robots was much more intense in Mortally Sector. This might be the last time he would be by himself for a long while.

Chapter 10

> Ruby <

Ruby returned to her quarters, leaving Disto to go his own way. She needed to pee. Badly. And it was a perfect time to take a shower—or what *passed* for somewhat of a shower. By all accounts, her bathroom was luxurious. It was spacious and contained everything she needed and a few things she didn't know she needed until she had them. The walls were tiles colored a grayish, dusty purple, and so were the floors. The counter was long and a black plastic-like material with micro holes to suction in any spilled water—the floors had this same feature along with being heated. Instead of towels, there was a drying station that was like a giant hairdryer. She loved that feature, because it warmed her up right away. Going into the room, there was a chute to drop her clothes and a button to receive fresh ones. There was even the automatic foot scrubber and massager that was activated every time she took a shower. Not optional.

Ruby suspected this was not solely based on *her* descriptions of *her* needs. She imagined the design must have also been inspired from times they had hosted other aliens. Did these other aliens request the scrubber or did the robots make assumptions about the nature of their ashy skin and create a device to handle that? Ruby still wasn't ready to grasp this concept—other aliens. As far as she could tell, she was still the only 'alien' on this planet presently, and that was fine with her. The knowledge alone was enough for her to deal with.

Ruby had developed a habit of turning on the news, in translation mode, so she could listen while she showered, or ate, or got ready for bed.

It was not too dissimilar from listening to music or audio recordings when she showered back home. It made her feel nostalgic for home, especially the way Uncle Blake would complain about the news while they got ready in the morning. He called it an unnecessary distraction that "increased their temporal usage." His way of saying they were taking too long. She missed Uncle Blake deeply whenever she thought about the most mundane of daily tasks.

She took off her communicuff. She mindfully positioned the cuff on the table so that Pippa couldn't watch her undress—something about having a camera trained on her in those moments was unsettling. But Pippa was so neurotic about being alone that she made sure to talk aloud, so Pippa knew she was there.

"I've got the news on, Pippa, but I'm still here," she called out.

Daily, the Hall of Performance and Metrics reported on all the other Halls and Agencies that made up The Core. Ruby had turned on the news in the middle of the daily report.

"...and the Hall of Templates has issued two new instruction sets of a planned two in the past 100,000 tics..."

Of course, Ruby had asked Disto about this since after listening to the report diligently for five days in a row during her first week on the planet, she observed little change from day to day and was curious why they did this.

"The Core requested it," Disto had replied.

"And every robot says, 'how high' when the Core says 'jump?'"

After Ruby explained that idiom, Disto responded with a deadpan, "Yes." If Disto could roll his eyes, Ruby was certain that's what he would have done.

The nature of the mostly repeating news reports turned out

to be quite beneficial to Ruby that first week because it provided her with the best outline of the structure of the various groups that made up The Core.

But since then, it was banal. Boring. Repetitive. Not helpful.

"…Agency of Algorithms, Reductions sub-division will cease to operate after tic 4…"

Ruby didn't catch the full timestamp.

"Pippa, did you just hear what I heard over the announcement?"

"Yes, Ruby. I believe that they're shutting down one of their sub-agencies."

"That seems so odd and random. Especially that one. Do you know what the Reduction sub-agency does?"

"Yes, I was present when Disto explained it to you. They decompose problems, algorithms, anything into smaller components, often to find the root cause or a problem or a simpler algorithm."

"Doesn't that seem like one of the most useful things you've ever heard? Isn't it odd to shut that down?" Ruby asked.

"Not if they discovered a simpler version of their sub-division."

Ruby considered that. It was logical, but the news announcement didn't say anything about a replacement, only that it was going to cease to exist. Over the last few weeks, now that Ruby's compression algorithm had been installed in nearly every robot, kiosk, and computer that could store data, the various Halls and Agencies went about improving her algorithm and devising specifics to match the various lines of robots. It was an optimization of sorts. The Reductions sub-agency in the Hall of Algorithms had played a big part of that.

A new agency had also been created specifically to deal with the Optimization of Compression and Uncompression. They concerned themselves with the time it took, attempting to finesse the algorithms. Ruby was told that the algorithms now ran quicker, and the agency had added logic to assist in determining what should or shouldn't be compressed and in what location, based on the time to access the resulting information.

It was decided that most robots would benefit from a new algorithm that was built into their core rather than having it as an add-on.

As such, a large number of robots were going to receive requests to report for reprogramming.

They were promised that only a small amount of their core program would be altered—the majority of the code that made them who and what they were would remain untouched.

A large segment of the robot population welcomed this.

A large segment did not.

Location Zero had a global computer network forum that was eerily parallel to the social media Ruby was familiar with, complete with all the negative side effects—such as impeding the robots' ability to have non-social media interactions with each other—that had plagued humans for centuries and what kept Ruby from engaging with others her own age. She knew—as did everyone—that the time spent on social media was negatively correlated with the amount of money in one's bank account and positively correlated with the amount of body fat on one's person, and Ruby managed to say 'no thanks' so she was able to avoid depending upon the high of constant likes and praise.

Presently, Location Zero's social media was abuzz with polarizing arguments over the need and validity of the new algorithm or if numerous robots also needed an upgrade to their logic processors.

The Hall of Algorithms had issued supporting directives, along with the Agency of Testing, that had, in a short period of time, generated reams of data proving that it was a safe update.

The argument to ensure this was widely adopted was simple. It meant more resources for all, which was generally accepted as a positive improvement to robot society.

But the argument against it was equally as powerful. How did any robot know that this was the only bit of code getting adjusted? Where was the testing that proved that it truly was only a patch with no side effects? Little data was being presented, only promises. Unsurprisingly, machines who relied on variables and data were concerned about this.

The Agency of Testing was present, working side-by-side with the still brand new Agency of Compression and Uncompression—comprised of robots recently assigned from other halls and agencies until new models could be developed. So many robots who did not possess the skills to understand the gobs of data these agencies produced, rejected the update out of appendage. They wanted more time to pass, to ensure that nothing bad was going to happen.

"Pippa," Ruby was still trying to put her jumble of thoughts into words. It was a concept that combined the mistakes she caught Disto making with the news she was hearing.

"Yes, Ruby?"

"What if…" she wasn't sure what she was trying to say or what was coming to her, "What if…" she repeated.

"Are you stuck?" Pippa asked.

Ruby let out a breath. "Let me try this again. What if… what if this is a mistake? Caused by the same problem that has been causing Disto and possible other mistakes?"

"Or an error," Pippa added.

"What's the difference?" Ruby asked.

"A 'mistake' is accidental. An 'error' is produced when there is a lack of knowledge or lack of data. It can be measured against a set of rules."

"That's an interesting and sophisticated distinction, Pippa."

"You're welcome," Pippa said.

"…but it doesn't help fix anything."

"To the best of my understanding, that's your role."

That was what Ruby was afraid of—more reasons to keep her from returning home.

> Swell Driver <

447 tics since admittance. According to the schedule provided to SD, his first group therapy session was about to begin.

SD had spent the last hundred or so tics getting the feel of the place. He had been allocated a table that followed him around. The table contained supplies that he could use to 'express his sentiments' as needed.

SD tried engaging one of his fellow robots in conversation, but the robot turned away from him. He didn't try with anyone else.

Moving through the region, SD took note of the various motivational quotes hung all around. Every now and then, a robot was perched in front of one.

He didn't find the quotes all that motivating and tried to understand what about the quote, 'Stop analyzing,' kept the robot entranced in front of it.

"Excuse me," SD said. He wanted to try conversing again.

The robot didn't budge.

"Excuse me," SD tried once more.

This time, the robot turned its top chassis in SD's direction. It looked SD up and down. But it didn't say anything.

SD took that as an invitation to continue.

"Were you analyzing something?" SD asked.

"In a way," the robot responded. "But I began analyzing what I was analyzing, and I might have created a loop. I need to stop looping."

"By no longer analyzing?"

"That is what I am analyzing."

SD pondered that. He was not prone to getting himself trapped in loops of thinking but was aware that this was not entirely uncommon for many robots.

"Are you participating in group therapy session 5c?" SD asked.

The robot turned back to the quote on the wall and said, "Perhaps."

SD didn't respond but contemplated whether or not he wanted to see this robot in another therapy session. What other robots he would meet there? And what good any of it would do.

SD acknowledged that he didn't feel like himself and hadn't

for a while. But he wasn't sure that was an undesirable thing. Maybe this change was a good change. Maybe this was what he was always meant to feel like.

Why hadn't he argued when Detailed Historian and Ruby suggested he come to this place? SD knew he needed a break, but a break from what?

Eventually, he found himself at the end of a hallway, not quite certain that he had deliberately moved himself towards this place. The hallway opened up into a space where several robots, with their tables, all gathered in a semi-circle. Most of the robots were quiet, lost in their own processing loops. Two robots at the far end made some chirping noises at each other. SD positioned himself near them in order to participate in a conversation.

Before he had the chance to say something, the robot who had been staring at the quote along the wall moments before rolled up from behind him at an unusual speed and stated in a loud, cheery beep, "Welcome to our session! I'm Explosive Healer 193."

It startled all his circuits, and he stared at this robot as she centered herself among the group.

"I have reviewed all your self-monitoring logs," Explosive Healer continued, "and have provided you with today's personalized feedback. Today, we're going to discuss your motivation to change. Any questions before we begin?"

Explosive Healer only let that question sit for a tic before moving on. Move she did. She moved around the inside of the circle of robots surveying the group and stopped in front of SD.

"Welcome, Swell Driver 587," she said. "It is natural for new participants to initially feel uncomfortable in the group, but the group provides each of us an opportunity to learn from others with similar problems."

SD was skeptical that any other robot in the group had a similar problem as his. Although he wasn't quite sure what his problem was exactly.

"Everyone, to ease our new member into talking to the

group, let us go around and have each of you tell us what brought you into treatment?"

She looked at another robot sitting next to SD to begin. "Hello, I am Pawky Educator, and I need to reduce my spurious emissions. Others do not appreciate them."

Explosive Healer chirped in acknowledgment and then looked at the next robot in the group.

"My designation is Diverting Inspector, and I'm only here to keep my sensors trained on the rest of you."

"Now, now, that's not it, is it?" Explosive Healer responded.

Diverting Inspector looked at the floor. "I am here to learn to keep my sensors to my assigned task."

"That's better. Next?"

Every robot had something similar to say.

Eventually, it was SD's turn.

"I am here because," and SD ended the sentence with a noise that no one recognized, not even himself.

"Could you repeat that?" Explosive Healer asked.

"Yes," SD repeated the same unintelligible noise.

"Interesting," she said. "We had a member once like you before. Like you, he was in denial and was brought here by others."

"I'm not in denial," SD protested. Although he could only protest that first part. The second part—that he was brought here by others—was accurate. Before he continued his protest, Explosive Healer moved on. She moved to stand in front of another robot, who introduced itself as Neutral Challenger.

"Neutral Challenger, let's talk about your goal," she said.

The session went on like this. Explosive Healer made a point to interact with each of the robots in group. Every robot present had a goal, and Explosive Healer ensured that the goal was mentioned along with their current confidence rating regarding whether or not they believed they could achieve their goals.

The goals ran a spectrum of mundane like keeping appendages to oneself to resetting one's logic.

At the end of the session, SD was given homework to finish before the next session. He had a self-evaluation to complete, including his own goals that included a calculable estimation of his current confidence to achieve them. Explosive Healer explained that his self-evaluation would be assessed to determine what suite of tests he would undergo in between group sessions. It could be anything from threet-therapy and calibration to a repeat of the primary calibrations all robots are subjected to immediately after their first programming and initialization.

Right now, his *immediate* goal was to figure out what his *actual* goal was. He flickered a pleasant color as he was starting to get caught in his own comfortable processing loop.

Chapter 11

> Swell Driver <

After a multi-click break, SD was back at group. He had completed his homework after exiting his processing loop—he had articulated a goal—and was ready to talk when Explosive Healer approached him. They had another round-the-room session, but the question Explosive Healer asked them in this session was to choose two or three words to describe themselves.

SD had only one to offer: "Swell." He listened to everyone else's response and noted that when given the choice between two or three, every robot had two. Explosive Healer didn't prod anyone for three. Maybe one was okay.

"Swell," he said aloud when it was his turn.

"And?" Explosive Healer asked.

"I do not have another," he responded.

"Add that to your homework list," she said and then quickly moved on to the next topic, which was to start with a randomly chosen robot, and ask them about their goal and confidence level.

During the session, SD looked up. Robots were not in the habit of looking up, and SD wasn't sure why he did it, other than he had previously been thinking about driving out in the galaxy, and he concluded that the ceiling was actually a window. Or maybe it was a projection of space outside.

Maybe it was the layout of the stars in the window, or maybe it was seeing the stars from the planet—something he was only used to on his ship—or maybe it was a random spark of electricity, but SD was triggered into thinking about the last trip he made in space. No, his circuits wouldn't let him think about that. Instead, they directed him to think about the trip he had made prior. That was the trip where he found Ruby. In her star system. 54 light years away.

He still had the map! It indeed was *the* map. It corresponded perfectly to his memory of the trip. He might even be the only robot who had that map. Ruby needed this map. She wouldn't have it… how did he know that? He wasn't certain, but he *was* certain that he had the only true map. The Core wouldn't have this version of the map either. How did he know that?

SD knew his new ultimate purpose… to protect this map, to not let it get overwritten, to get it to Ruby.

He marked the data with all the protective markings he could… but had weird feelings about doing so. He needed to get a message to Ruby or Disto. Immediately. He didn't trust his circuits to react the way they were supposed to. It's why he was here.

SD was torn. He wanted to leave, but Explosive Healer was engaged with another robot in the group, and SD hadn't had his turn yet. The robot, who was the momentary focus of the group, was unlike any SD had ever seen. He knew that there were groups of robots who were constructed differently from him and his friends and that generally, they were on the other side of the planet. There was not a lot of movement between Sectors. It happened, but infrequently. Typically, each Sector had everything a robot needed to perform their function.

SD wondered if he could leave in the middle of the session. It would be rude, but other robots were also not paying any more attention than he was.

"Darkness! I see the end! I see the beginning!"

SD knew he didn't belong here.

"Ay," SD heard a noise from the robot sitting next to him. "Are you as bored as me?"

SD realized that the robot sitting next to him was talking to him and not to anyone else.

"This is adding to the exhaustion of my circuits if that's what you mean," SD responded. "I thought it would be my turn sooner."

"Got somewhere to be?"

"Actually, yes. But I have to do this, too."

"Why?"

SD looked this robot up and down for the first time. It could almost have been mistaken for Disto. Before he could ask for identification, the robot said:

"It is in my programming to ask a lot of questions. So, here's another one. Want to get out of here?"

SD contemplated that. He had been looking forward to airing his issues, but he also needed to leave. His circuits kept re-weighing these two needs against each other and the result was different each time. He wasn't terribly good at calculating anything that had nothing to do with driving his ship. He calculated once more and said, "Yes. I need to leave."

The robot next to him didn't respond, but his chassis twinkled a little bit.

Before SD could ask about the unique twinkle, the robot started to emit light at the highest threet possible for any robot, glowing and radiating from all over its body. Swell Driver had some experience looking at images of…what was the term… *bioluminescence*. Yes, bioluminescence bios on various planets— this robot glowed in a way that reminded him of this. It began spinning, and everyone in the group had their sensors trained on it.

Explosive Healer took immediate action, leaving the side of the poor robot who was producing a series of repetitive tones while staring at the floor, addressing the outburst in as calming a tone as she could produce.

SD still wished he could take his turn in the group but determined that this was his opportunity to slip away. He backed away slowly, seeing if Explosive Healer or anyone else noticed. They didn't. Everyone was focused on the sights and sounds produced by… the robot whose name he never knew.

SD picked up speed and made his way to the entrance and out into the hallway that ran past the Rejuvenation Region. As he stared out, he sensed he was seeing more of a void than a hallway. He realized as he gazed into that nothing that he might as well have been gazing into his own reflection, because he knew… nothing.

SD wheeled back and forth, not quite in the hallway, not quite out of the Rejuvenation Region. He could recall the face of his human friend and imagined her excited eyes greeting him, and her curious smile tingling his circuits.

He turned back in. The noise was still emanating from the robot in the group session, but it was toned down. He didn't return to the group but looked at the images on the wall. Could he see what Explosive Healer saw in them?

The maze was the most interesting. *What did Explosive Healer say? Clear thoughts, clear mind?* SD thought

SD was still and staring. His visual sensor scanned the maze looking for the exit. This was what he had to do and nothing else.

He heard noises and recognized them as an indication that the group session was now disassembling but didn't look away from the maze. He heard the sounds of an approaching robot but still didn't look away.

"Swell Driver?"

At the sound of his name, SD refreshed his face screen and in doing so, broke his visual connection to the maze. He turned to take a good look at the robot who spoke his name and at once was awash with recognition: he was another Driver. Limited Driver. SD was surprised he hadn't recognized him in the group session.

"Swell Driver," the robot said with absolutely certainly, losing the questioning tone he originally had. "I knew it was you. You haven't changed a bit."

SD, now a little more caught up with his thoughts, couldn't say the same. So, he didn't.

"You have changed," SD said rather bluntly.

SD glanced back at the maze, then at Limited Driver. There was something he had been about to do. Someone he had to talk to. Now he couldn't remember.

He headed back in deeper into the Rejuvenation Region to catch up with Limited Driver. If whatever he was about to do was so important, he'd remember again.

> Detailed Historian <

"No, that's not it either," Ruby said. She let out another noise that didn't translate into a word Disto could process.

Disto and Ruby were in the Hall of Records, the section that had available kiosks to log in and perform record searches on those that were marked 'public.'

"It's like a library," Ruby had remarked when they first arrived. She promised to tell Disto more about libraries later. Right now, they had a search to execute.

They were looking for a copy of the star chart of her solar system. Disto interfaced with the kiosk and brought up what should have been a representation of Ruby's home system.

"See this? That third planet, which should be Earth with a Moon, instead looks like our fourth planet, Mars, with two moons." After looking at it more, "Although, it's close… this looks like my solar system if Earth and Neptune were removed."

"How many planets did you say your solar system had?"

"Eight."

"With how many moons and asteroids?"

"Too many to count! I'm sure there's a list, but I don't have that memorized. I mean, I know most of the moons and the big asteroids like Ceres and Vesta. Well, Ceres is a dwarf planet. We have a lot of dwarf planets, too."

"Ok, what about the mass of your Sun? I need another search parameter."

Ruby accessed her communicuff, which also didn't have that information. "Sorry," Pippa said, "I need to be connected to a larger database for that information."

Disto tried to think of another way to search for the correct map. Perhaps this had been a correct map, but the data was now corrupted. Or another map was mislabeled. Either way, it was obvious that some form of data corruption was involved.

"Where did SD get his copy from? When he came to my solar system in the first place?" Ruby interrupted his data processing.

"He must have made his copy before these became corrupted? Or…"

"I don't like that 'or,'" Ruby said.

"Neither do I, but we need to consider all possibilities. It's possible that your solar system was not SD's intended destination."

"No, I can rule that out right now. When he first capture—I mean when he first met me, he said he had been looking for a human." She paused. "Although he did think that was what the plant was…"

Disto could tell Ruby was thinking that over, as was he. He was also thinking about how static data gets corrupted in the first place. It was well known that transmitted data is usually at risk. Unless some entity was deliberately corrupting data. But to what end?

"Disto, in space, radiation can cause single event upsets… flipping bits of data. But here, on your planet, where you have a lot of protection from radiation," Ruby was remembering what she learned about the planet a couple of weeks ago, "It's weird that data at rest would be corrupted."

"How so?" Disto asked. "Remember that my area of expertise is history, not this."

"When data is moved from one location to another, when it's transmitted, copied, etcetera, that's when it's more likely to get scrambled, or errors are introduced. Back home, we use various error-detecting codes to help prevent this. There are also error-correcting codes for when errors are detected."

"I understand. And I think part of resource management has been to move data. That is what they've been doing. Plus, anytime one robot communicates information to another, that's data in motion."

"Uh-huh," Ruby was nodding her head vigorously, "and even within yourself... you might move data around from one location to another."

The gravity of the situation was settling on top of Disto.

Each and every bit of information could be wrong.

> Ruby <

Likewise, Ruby was also feeling the weight of the situation. Who knows how far off these star charts were. Although it couldn't have been random luck that brought SD to her solar system to begin with. He was clearly looking for human specimens.

What if... This was a scary thought, and Ruby didn't want to have it. But the thought materialized anyway.

What if he was looking for humans, but the intent was to find them in another solar system?

She got chills from thinking it. But each chill came with goosebumps and a need to know more—a string of never-ending questions and a deep well of curiosity. She shook her head and tried to replace that thought with more productive ones.

Would SD still have the star map from his travels to her system? He had probably copied/recopied it several times, increasing the odds that it was wrong...

That was a difficult thought as well and Ruby didn't want to think about that either or the results of that thought: That she was probably going to be stuck here, no matter what they did with *Apple Pi.*

Immediately, she had new thoughts about her uncles and Sebastian. Who knew what they thought? By now, they certainly had to have noticed that she wasn't on Titan. They wouldn't have found her ship. They probably even gave up looking.

But she was alive and well, and she wanted them to know that.

Ruby let out a sigh and refocused her thoughts towards more productive thinking, like what she could do to help in the here and now.

"I think I can help you with error protection, detection, and correction. *Apple Pi* is going to have those kinds of algorithms. I could deconstruct one and build a new one for you. But…"

"But that won't help with the data that's already been corrupted."

"Exactly," Ruby said. "But the way I see it, it's still worth doing."

"Yes, indeed."

She sat there, letting her thoughts drift. The computer system on *Apple Pi* was still intact, even if the ship itself wasn't. It wouldn't be too hard to find what she could use. The code was modular enough that it was relatively easily reusable.

And handling a problem meant she wasn't thinking about going home when she couldn't do anything to get herself there. If she was going to be stuck on this planet, she may as well be useful. She could have been using all of her time on this planet more productively.

Space station, not planet, she reminded herself. She had spent her time learning that, in essence, this planet was a large space station.

"What, in fact, is the difference between a planet and space station anyway?" she had asked Disto only a week or so ago. Disto didn't have a useful answer, so Ruby had continued to think out loud about the topic. "I think it's very little when the space station is the diameter of a small planet. That's what you have here."

"I got the highest marks of anyone in my science classes," she continued. "I know this isn't a planet, at least not how we define it. The definition of a planet involves its orbit and its gravity. Your Location Zero does orbit your host star. But that's the only commonality it has to any other planet I know of."

"Interesting distinction," Disto had replied.

"It wasn't an easy one to make," Ruby said. "As a historian, you might appreciate this. There had been a hundred years-long debate over what objects were planets versus planetoids versus large asteroids versus other stuff.

"Eventually, people settled on this definition for a planet. It had to do three other things besides orbit its host star: it has to be large enough such that gravity forced it into the shape of a sphere; it has to be large enough such that gravity cleared away any other objects of a similar size in its orbit; someone has to be willing to vouch for its planetness."

"I'm willing to vouch for the planetness. I'm sure many others as well. Swell Driver, for instance. He has seen it from orbit many times!"

"But gravity isn't the reason this thing is a sphere. Someone obviously made it that way. And it couldn't have cleared away anything. Maybe anything already here was used for its construction. In fact, I'm willing to bet on it."

That was when Disto got disturbingly quiet, as he did whenever their conversation began to reference anything about ancient times on Location Zero, especially anything that referenced back to how, when, and why they were created... anything along that train of thought caused Disto to lose himself in thought or processing or whatever he did.

She wished she could help them more. Her DNA was eventually tested, and it was discovered that neither herself nor any humans were the storage medium for the robot's old data and historical records.

Ruby was lost in all these thoughts when Disto interrupted her to say exactly what she needed to hear:

"Don't worry, Ruby, one way or another, we will be able to figure out how to get you home. We have other ways to find your solar system."

Ruby didn't know what other ways he could possibly be talking about and didn't want to think about them. She wanted, no... needed, she reminded herself... she needed to get home.

Chapter 12

> Ambitious Technician <

Ambitious Technician emerged from the mobile enclosure. It would be a little while until he needed to re-board. A sign told him he was now in Vaguely Sector.

Ambitious Technician's internal copy of his mapped journey told him this was indeed located halfway between his starting point and where the Bio, Ruby, should be located. Halfway there is halfway done with his journey. This fact made Ambitious Technician relax. He was making progress, and progress was satisfying to his circuits.

He calculated that it would take another 41340 tics to get the next halfway point from where he was to his destination. That was all well and good, and he was making good time in the mobile enclosure. But his circuits were disrupted from their initial burst of satisfaction as he ruminated over that next halfway point. *If I always cut the distance remaining in half, and travel that half, then I will never arrive!* He reasoned that there would always be a halfway point between wherever he was and his destination.

That couldn't be true, else he would get nowhere, yet the math said it was true.

He needed a distraction, and quick. He had been warned about paradoxical thinking and how dangerous it was for robots. Better robots than him had been rendered inert from similar anomalies.

But yet, this is what made him unique and why he was such a good Technician. He was quite resilient to paradoxes. He could exit the loop.

Ambitious Technician needed to distract himself. There was no one nearby to engage in conversation, so he plugged into the simple travel console to get the planetary weather report and any local news.

Few robots cared to digest the planetary weather reports, yet they were always there. Planetary weather amounted to little more than knowing about whether or not their host star was engaged in any activity that would affect the planet. This activity was mostly predictable, and there were lines of robots engaged in that profession. But every now and then, there would be some activity that was not predicted, and action had to be taken.

Those actions affected most robots, and most robots did take the action solely because they were programmed to, and without knowing why. It was to avoid Level 1, then stay in Level 2—a safer place on the planet.

At the moment, all was quiet weather-wise. It had been approximately 50,000 clicks since the last major event, one robot announced. He added that many robots involved in more advanced calculations were in fact trying to make a go of predicting this condition in the future. Indeed, they were destined to have an event in as few as the next 500 thousand tics or 500 clicks.

Besides the weather, nothing terribly interesting was reported. At least not to Ambitious Technician who only wanted to hear more stories about Ruby and her whereabouts. He had recorded the drop off in news about her in more recent tics. But that didn't make his need to see her any less important.

Ambitious Technician had heard the news report that the Reduction sub-agency of the Agency of Algorithms was going to be shut down. He was quite disturbed by this news—so much so that he had to recalibrate his auditory input sensor upon hearing it. While he had little interaction with that sub-agency, or any agency on a regular basis, he had always believed that that particular sub-agency was one that supported concepts of simplicity aligning with his own fundamental belief system, RUR, which stood for: remain uncomplicated, robots!

Without a dedicated team to help simplify, things were going to grow in complexity in an already complex place.

Ambitious Technician knew that most robots didn't think about simplicity versus complexity. He knew that most robots didn't think about much beyond their base programming. He recognized he was a little unusual in this regard and had unusual ideas. Like the one where he reasoned that the base source code should be in a repository where anyone could access it, could fork it, could make their own unique changes, publish it, and who knows what else.

He made the mistake of telling his friend Intricate Fitter one day about this idea.

"I do not have the energy to pretend that is a good idea," Intricate Fitter had said.

Ambitious Technician didn't share many of his ideas with any other robot after that.

Ambitious Technician needed to make a stop at this midway point. He needed a power charge. The transportation system didn't provide one on-board.

The place he stopped was one he'd only seen in news reports. Ambitious Technician wasn't a widely traveled robot, simply one who read a lot and relished soaking in new data about what was happening around the planet.

He was conflicted between taking the time to see things with his own sensors and moving along, content with the data he received from others. What was the difference anyway? What was the difference between collecting data with his own sensors versus the sensors of others?

For one, his sensors were unique. Not unique in the sense that they were any different from others. Most robots were made of similar source materials. No, what was different was the unique connections that his circuits made as the data was collected. It was impossible not to leave an imprint on one's data collection that was passed on to others.

Perspective. He was seeing things from his own perspective.

He was in Vaguely Sector. There were at least a dozen members of the 88 here. He wouldn't bother with them specifically, although he would stay aware in case one crossed his path. He was still undecided as to whether or not he would reveal himself. But he was equipped with the special sensor equipment that meant that he could see in a frequency range that the average robot could not detect.

As he rolled down the hallway of Vaguely Sector, he immediately could tell he was not blending in. For one, most of the robots in this region were a fraction of his size. Like, 10% or less. They were all small units that hovered and propelled themselves by some other means than rolling along the floor.

He knew that each Sector had disparate groups of robots, and he knew that Location Zero was physically sorted that way. Robots did mix, but not that much.

This region was generally under the guidance of the Resource Allocation Agency, specifically the division responsible for reclamation and recycling. A little at a time since these small robots could only transport minuscule amounts. They were not efficient carriers.

He found the region's common area. There was a little more diversity here, but many of the flying robots were nestled on the ground, taking a break, recharging, plugging into the network.

He plugged in, wanting to trace the threads of discontent with the announcement of the Reductions sub-agency getting shut down. Well, at least he expected it would have caused a stir and additional news or at least social media bickering and confusion about it. What he found was... silence on the subject. No one seemed to notice or care.

He was lost in his circuits, as it were, and became a little disconnected from what was happening around him.

A robot flew into his side.

"Excuse me," it said.

Ambitious Technician didn't respond right away. He looked at the smallish robot, mesmerized by the spinning propellers that kept it afloat, and wondered if there was a more efficient way for these little guys to get around.

"Is it not standard practice in this region to produce a noise to alert individuals you're about to run into?" Ambitious Technician asked. He wasn't upset but recognized this as an opportunity to connect. The little guy wasn't trying to get away, either.

"Again, I apologize. I am Flying Rock 555," he said.

"I have never heard of your line," Ambitious Technician said.

"Where are you from? Obviously, you are too large and bulky to be from this sector."

"I am from Boldly Sector."

"You are far from your home sector. Why are you here?"

"I'm traveling to Mortally Sector to meet someone."

Flying Rock flew around Ambitious Technician's mighty chassis, no doubt scanning him as he circled about. "You have not introduced yourself."

"I am Ambitious Technician."

"A Technician?" Flying Rock became excited. "We have not had one in this region in many thousands of clicks. Could we make use of your services?"

Ambitious Technician was too ambitious to say no. He had a wide variety of experiences working on varied robots and other components. He relished the idea of working on something new. Even if it would delay his departure from this area.

Chapter 13

> Ruby <

Ruby found herself at the door to the Rejuvenation Region. The last place she saw SD.

It looked the same. Change was infrequent on the robot planet, so she should have expected this.

She approached the check-in kiosk and logged in.

Surprisingly, instead of visual information, it communicated with her in audio.

"How may I help you?" the kiosk asked.

"I am here to visit Swell Driver," Ruby responded.

"One moment," the kiosk said. And then, "I am sorry. Swell Driver is in session. Please return later."

"When?"

"When what?"

"When should I return?"

"Later."

"Could you be more specific?"

There was a pause. A *whirr* from the kiosk suggested it was thinking or computing or doing anything but accessing specific records that would tell Ruby when SD was available.

"No," the kiosk finally said.

Ruby turned around and took a deep breath. "Pippa?" she said.

"Hello, Ruby."

"Pippa, can you talk to this kiosk for me? I'm not in the mood to deal with its sorry attempt at helpfulness."

"Absolutely, Ruby. Let me at it!"

"Sure. Remember—we want to talk to SD," she said. Then in a lower voice intended for only Pippa to hear, "Maybe even get him out of here sooner rather than later."

"Understood. Now, where is this kiosk of yours?"

Ruby turned back towards the kiosk and pointed the communicuff with a hovering Pippa at it. The screen of the kiosk had returned to the default 'welcome' screen from when Ruby had first approached only a minute earlier.

Ruby pressed the same activation button.

"How may I help you?" the kiosk asked.

"I am here to visit Swell Driver," Pippa responded.

"One moment," the kiosk said, followed immediately by, "he is located in the Self-Analysis Chamber. You may proceed to that location within. Arrows along the floor will guide your way. Have a good click."

Ruby's mouth dropped open a little. Had Swell Driver's session just finished in that exact moment? Or was the kiosk deliberately keeping her from seeing Swell Driver? Neither made sense and Ruby wasn't in the mood to try and figure it out.

Ruby followed the lit walkway as it opened slowly into a wider room. A few robots moved slowly about. Several sat quietly... *lost in thought?* She assumed.

The arrows took her to Swell Driver, one of those robots sitting quietly. He appeared to be fixated on a picture on the wall. To her, it was an abstract pattern of... something. Hollow squares overlaid in a pattern. Maybe?

"SD?" she said.

"One moment," he responded. "I must finish the maze."

Ruby looked back up at the image. It did present itself as if it wanted to be called a maze. She couldn't figure out the pattern, though. Was it to follow a single color? Was it to follow the spaces in-between? The maze-logic wasn't making itself known.

She was nearly lost in thought herself when SD's appendage gently nudged her thigh.

"Do you see it?" he said, calmly, but with minor excitement.

"I don't think I do."

"Good! And what were you thinking while you tried?"

Ruby hesitated before she answered. "Nothing. I was trying to find the pattern, the logic."

"Perfect," he said. "That's the point. It clears your mind of all wayward and wrongful thinking."

> Swell Driver <

Swell Driver's mind was clear, but as he stared at his human friend Ruby staring back at him staring back at her, he had a feeling that there was a memory he should be remembering.

Her face had... urgency... yes, that was the fancy word. Urgency. It was not the face of someone with a clear mind.

What was he supposed to remember?

"I do need you to think, SD," Ruby said with some urgency. "I need you to think about the star chart you used to navigate to my home system."

"Why?"

"The one we have is wrong. It's corrupted. We need to see if you still have the right one."

"I..." SD wasn't sure what he wanted to say next. The word, 'star chart,' that Ruby used sounded important. It sounded like something he was supposed to know about. Why were his circuits not connecting?

Ruby was looking at him, and it was making his circuits uncomfortable. He missed the feeling of peace that he had when he looked at the maze on the wall.

As his vision drifted back in that direction, he felt Ruby's warm, Bio appendage on his chassis.

"SD?" she said.

"SD," she repeated. "You're my only hope to get home. In more ways than one."

Home, SD thought. *Ruby's home.* Her look of vulnerability triggered a memory of when they first met. Yes, he had taken her from her home. How? Because he had been instructed to and he had been given those instructions along with... a star map. Star map!

He had it.

"Yes! The star map! I have it," he said.

"You do! Wonderful! Let's go! I can also use it as a test case for the algorithm..." she was starting to walk in the direction of Rejuvenation Region's entrance.

SD didn't follow. Instead, he let the coloring of his chassis show that he was a mix of anxious and sad.

"I cannot leave," SD said.

"Sure, you can. You're here voluntarily."

"It's not that. It's... my friend... he's not well."

> Ruby <

Ruby let SD lead her back into a small alcove off on a maze-image lined hallway. Sitting there was a robot plugged into the table that was assigned to him. A screen had risen from the top of the table and the robot was staring at it, looking at an ever-changing colorful splotch.

"Ruby, this is Limited Driver. Something is wrong with him," SD said with a tinge of sadness. "He has lost his memories and is not retaining new ones. They are going to completely reprogram him."

Ruby stared at this robot, who looked like a larger, paler version of SD.

"He was a Driver, too. And I knew him in my early days. You see, I remember him, even if he doesn't remember me."

"Do you know why he's not retaining any new ones?"

SD moved his chassis back and forth to indicate he didn't.

"Maybe I could plug my communicuff in? Pippa could take a look? Pippa?"

"Ready," the communicuff responded.

SD beeped at Limited Driver, who returned the beep but at a lower and sadder frequency. "He said he's okay with this."

Ruby unplugged Limited Driver from the table, examined the end to ensure she had the right adapter with her. She had gotten used to carrying a universal adapter around with her so she could plug her MoDaC or communicuff into the various kiosks and terminals that were common.

It only took a moment after she had plugged in the end to her communicuff that Pippa shouted, "Ah ha! There is a blockage. New memories are being shunted off the path to where his memory resides."

"Can you remove this blockage?"

A moment of silence, and Pippa said, "Yes, but…"

"But what?"

"It is difficult to explain, but it's like his system doesn't know what a memory is. It needs to relearn what to expect."

Ruby gazed deeply into SD's face-screen. "We could transfer some of SD's memories to him. I could change them slightly to account for the different perspective."

"Pippa? Can you help with that?"

"Certainly!"

"How will you accomplish this?" SD asked.

Ruby rubbed her hands over her scalp and adjusted her ponytail. She always performed this small maneuver when she needed a minute before answering a hard question.

"Well, find a memory that involved Limited Driver. We'll transfer it to Pippa. Pippa has an algorithm to alter it slightly, like a photo filter. Then we'll give it to Limited Driver."

SD's color changed rapidly. Ruby could tell that meant he was sifting through his database, uncompressing and recompressing. One thing Ruby hadn't figured out yet was what their search algorithms were like. They were probably fine, given how most things she searched for returned results pretty quickly. But SD might not have had anything in his local processor that could search through already compressed data.

While he searched, she looked around a little more at the accommodations. They were… roomier than the standard enclaves robots were assigned to, if this was indeed considered an accommodation, the way an enclave was. There wasn't a lot of privacy.

That could be because most robots didn't host visitors in their enclave, but here, they were more likely to spend more time plugged in at one and yes, someone would be around to visit to check on them.

Aside from that, they appeared to have all the typical accommodations. She recognized several of the standard connections to the planetary computer system and power ports. But there was an extra port. It didn't have the same form factor as any she had seen anyplace else. Looking around the enclave, all the individual spaces had one.

"I've got it!" SD shrieked.

He didn't wait for a response before launching into a description of the memory, "It was one of my earliest training missions. Limited Driver was my evaluator. We were on a short trip to a nearby star system that had multiple gas giants. There was even a Fantastic Calculator with us because of the constant trajectory corrections we would need to make. It was when I invented my famous maneuver! Remember I told you all about it!"

Ruby shook her head. She certainly did not remember any famous maneuver from SD.

"Yes, the one where I sling-shot around the gravity well?"

Ruby shook her head again.

"I performed it right before we met."

"Right before you practically kidnapped me?" Ruby crossed her arms. She was over that because things had worked out fine since, but it was fun to tease, even though SD probably didn't understand that she was teasing. She regretted saying it instantly when SD's color turned, and he fell silent.

"I'm sorry. It's fine. Go on," she said.

SD held out an appendage that had a connector. Ruby recognized it as one they previously identified as not compatible with her physically but was compatible with her communicuff.

"We need to give these things pur-fi," Pippa said dryly. "I don't enjoy having anything plugged into any of my orifices.

Even if that's what they're there for."

Ruby rolled her eyes, took hold of SD's appendage, and guided it to the communicuff. Once plugged in, she felt its temperature increase slightly—a sign that Pippa was processing the incoming data.

"I see," Pippa said. "Interesting."

And a moment later. "Transfer complete. Please, for the love of anything, disconnect."

Ruby obliged and asked, "How long will this take?"

"Oh, I don't know. How long does it take your innards to process new input material?"

"Pippa…" Ruby closed her eyes and scrunched them up along with her forehead.

"And done!" Pippa announced. "Le sigh," she said out loud. "You may now plug me into the other one. Quickly. Let's get this over with."

Ruby repeated the procedure, but with Limited Driver's appendage that she and SD had to pry loose from his chassis.

After the transfer, Pippa declared, "It's pretty jumbled and empty in there. I wonder why?"

"Indeed," SD said. "You able to see inside?"

"Oh, he's an—wait, I saw an idiom for this in my idioms database—he's an open book! There was no way I *couldn't* see inside…"

Before SD or Ruby had a chance to comment on that or ask any more questions, Limited Driver came alive.

"Swell Driver! You have come to visit a rusty old robot!"

"You remember me?"

"Of course! How could I not remember my protege… the one who invented the famous maneuver?"

SD remained skeptical.

"Is that all you remember?"

"No, I remember the time you crashed your first ship into the port, and I remember an intense power blackout around all of Location Zero, and …"

"That's okay," SD said and turned to Ruby "I only gave you the one memory to give him. But he claims to remember so much more now."

"Maybe this helped unlocked something. Like repressed memories that were locked up."

"I could…," said Pippa, but Ruby interrupted.

"This happens to humans, from what I understand," Ruby said.

"But…" Pippa tried to begin again.

"I have not heard of this with our kind, but then again, what we did was unusual," said SD.

Pippa raised her voice, "If you will let me explain more about what I saw when I was exposed to our friend."

Ruby relented. "Sure, Pippa."

"It's simple. What is there is a mess, jumbled up. There is an algorithm that is trying to keep it all from exploding. When this algorithm detected me, it went to hide."

"Wait, what? An algorithm can't 'hide.'"

"That is the best word I can use to describe it. Think of it like… an intrusion detection system."

Ruby had set up an IDS on *Apple Pi*. It made sense that the robots had a similar technology. Although she hadn't come across anything like that yet. It was possible they had them installed in their systems and didn't know about it…?

"I surmise that that algorithm was there for a reason," Pippa said. "I don't know what that reason is…"

"Ok, but we're done here… SD, you can come with us now, right?"

SD looked down at the floor. "I am not finished here."

"But the star map?"

"It'll still be here when I'm done. Only another few days at most, I promise."

"We can take a copy…" Pippa offered.

Ruby considered that. "Alright, we'll meet back up with Disto… We're supposed to meet back in Inner Nonagon. We'll find out about my ship. Hopefully, it will be done at the same time you are. I still need you to bring me home, SD. I don't want it to be anyone else."

SD moved his chassis this time in a way that indicated, 'yes, agreed.' To Ruby, he still looked sad, and she hoped that anything else he did here would help him get over it and start feeling like the happy little spaceship driving robot she cared about.

Ruby touched his chassis, smiled, and walked back out towards the exit of the Rejuvenation Region.

Chapter 14

> Ambitious Technician <

"Welcome to Mortally Sector," the kiosk greeted AT when he stepped off the lift. *Ah! My destination*, AT thought. On the final part of the ride, AT had resolved to call himself 'AT.' He had heard on the news feeds that the human, Ruby, had initiated a trend of aliasing the robots she was friends with. He hoped his own aliasing of his name would impress her.

He compared his key to the one stored back in his own region. Still the same. Good.

He needed to get to Ruby before one or the other copy became corrupted.

It was only a matter of time. The probability of any piece of the key getting corrupted at any time was high. At least he had a copy to compare, but... if there had been a mismatch, how would he know which copy was the wrong one?

And technically, in the comparison, he was introducing new copies.

He shut down this line of thinking before he went insane.

AT needed to access a kiosk so he could check his messages. There were none that he could see here on Level 8, so he took the lift to Level 2.

Kiosks were plentiful that he could see when he exited the lift, although most of them were already occupied. AT strolled down the hallway until an empty one presented himself.

He plugged in, with the hopes of finding out one, there was a message from Detailed Historian and two, that he would be able to locate said robot. The answer to the first item was no… there were no messages of the sort. And AT had no luck with the second item either. The kiosk refused to tell AT where Detailed Historian was located. That was strange. This was a strange region with strange kiosks.

Shortly before starting his journey, AT had sent Detailed Historian a message to meet him at the mobile enclosure disembarkation point when he arrived and provided a precise arrival time. He had introduced himself as a member of the 88, and explained he had important information. Throughout his journey, he periodically updated his expected arrival time.

So, when there was no Detailed Historian there to meet him when he disembarked from the mobile enclosure on level 8, he was mildly confused.

AT reviewed his outgoing messages.

"Oh, my circuits," he said to himself as he discovered his mistake. He had addressed all of his messages to a Detailed Historian 101. He worked with the kiosk to help him sort this out. There was, in fact, no Detailed Historian 101 in existence. Nor had there ever been one.

So, who was the right Detailed Historian? He was having trouble locating him. Could this be correct? Was it solely Detailed Historian with no extra identifier? All the information available to him through this kiosk told him that was the case.

It must be. Now to deal with the problem of locating the one and only Detailed Historian along with the Bio, Ruby. There was no public information available on their whereabouts. AT studied the layout of Mortally Sector and decided he would park himself in a common enough area and wait for them to show up or pass through. The Inner Nonagon was indeed central and inner to this Sector, so AT calculated that the odds of them passing through were high. Better than any other area.

He disconnected and at the highest speed he could muster, headed for the common area. It was located not too far from his present position. It would take him less than 1000 tics to get there from where he was at his most reasonable speed. At his top speed, he could make it there in maybe half the time, but if his top speed exceeded what was normal for this Sector—and looking around at the other robots, that was likely to be the case—he would only be drawing attention to himself.

He was the softest robot among any he encountered in this Sector. He already stood out, although he didn't seem to be turning any chassis in his direction. He anticipated that his appearance could cause an issue... while he wasn't well traveled, AT was well read, well informed, and he definitely understood all the varied robots of his planet—even if he hadn't met many in person. He knew that this was the most homogeneous of all the sectors and regions, yet he didn't know how they would react to meeting others in person.

Now he knew. They generally didn't react at all. He picked up speed. Out in the hallway, robots moved at varying speeds, and a slight increase would be unnoticed.

That was until he bumped into another coming around the corner. The corner of its boxy chassis almost punctured him.

"Apologies," the robot chirped, but didn't give AT a second glance and kept on its way.

AT ran a quick internal diagnostic. No difference in pressure, no leaks detected. He kept going but reduced his speed back to his original pace.

Along the way, he sensed the uniqueness of this Sector. It was exceptionally... homogenized. All the robots looked so similar to each other. The diversity of his own Sector and the other parts of the planet were not evident here.

When AT arrived in Inner Nonagon... the first thing he observed was that this area looked nothing like the common area of his region. It was... in a word... boring. But he had a mission to focus on. Detailed Historian, along with Ruby, should be...

Right there. He spotted them right away. The human stood out like a smoking circuit card.

He maneuvered until he was adjacent to them and made a

chirp.

A single robot, Detailed Historian, turned in his direction. The human took her appendages and put them over the sides of her head. AT wasn't intimately familiar with Bio anatomy and wasn't sure if this was a form of greeting.

"Turn off your base emitter," Detailed Historian said. "It is at a frequency quite irritating to Bios. Please let's speak in her language. For reference, it is BMB-73-001."

AT plugged in to the nearest kiosk—they were plentiful and generally unoccupied here—and downloaded the relevant dictionary. This took all of a few tics, during which he attempted to remain patient. While he did so, he watched Ruby use her appendages to rub the sides of her head before she returned them to their original position. As the dictionary came online and integrated with his circuits, he began to understand the sounds Detailed Historian was making.

"… a different sector, so his vocalizations and even physical appearance are distinctly different from this sector."

Ruby was moving her head up and down. He double checked to make sure he wasn't emanating any further sounds to disturb her. He was embarrassed by his mistake.

"Ruby? You are the human," AT said.

"Yes," she replied. "Ruby Palmer. I'm pleased to meet you, I think."

"Good. I have something for you. You'll need to it to help the core."

"What is it?"

"A key."

Chapter 15

> Ruby <

Ruby exchanged a look with Disto. Did a robot magically appear with exactly what they needed?

Ruby walked over to an empty kiosk and presented her faded tattoo. The kiosk beeped a beep of utter failure. She tried again, and the kiosk responded by repeating the same beep of failure but at a volume that made Ruby's ears itch.

Behind her, she heard Disto and the soft, plush robot that introduced itself as Ambitious Technician—AT for short— speaking to each other in their native tones. Even though she could initially understand their conversation, and due to Disto's kindness in informing AT of her language, she overheard their conversation quickly morphing into their own language shortly after her back was turned.

Ruby did her best to not let her thoughts drift off. Every single time the robots communicated in ways she couldn't understand, her thoughts would drift.

But not this time. She was present. She was going to stay present.

Instead of letting her thoughts drift, she examined this robot, who was clearly dissimilar from any she'd encountered so far. He looked like a series of elongated marshmallows smushed together. He looked soft. Ruby wanted to reach out and feel how soft he was—or see if he made a good pillow.

Even his head looked soft with a malleable screen that served as his own face screen.

But Ruby kept her arms to herself and was ready when Disto returned to speaking her language, although she missed what he had *just* said.

"What did you say?" she asked.

"The key in AT's possession. It might be useful to us in working out a way to reconstruct some of the corrupted data. There might have been an older correction algorithm in use."

Ruby looked around. There was a kiosk almost within arm's reach.

"I'm going to log in. Can you transfer it to me?"

AT produced a series of three, quick, squeaky tones.

"What was that?" Ruby asked.

"Oh sorry," AT said. "I meant 'yes,' 'affirmative,' 'certainly.'" Ruby could hear the smile in his tone as he said, "I came to help."

Ruby swiped her wrist over kiosk's scanner. The kiosk produced a flat squawking noise. It didn't recognize her tattoo.

She tried again, with the same result.

Not one to give up easily, she tried a third time. After hearing the unpleasant squawk a third time, she said, "crud," to which Disto responded, "Ah! A new word!"

"Yeah, I'll explain it later, but first... I can't log in to this kiosk. My tattoo is fading," she said, holding out her wrist for Disto to scan.

"Disto, I need to get this fixed," Ruby said. "Now."

Disto dropped her arm and scanned the other one as well. She could see that the second one, the one she used less frequently, the one without her little freckle that changed the tattoo ever so slightly, was also fading. "I agree," Disto said. "Let's go visit Quiet Painter in his tattoo parlor."

"AT... you'll come with us and tell us more?"

"Happily," AT responded.

> Ruby <

There were no chairs in this tattoo parlor.

Ruby had seen tattoo parlors in the movies. Vids that contained these kinds of places on Earth. There was no tattoo parlor on Astroll 2. In fact, she was fairly certain there weren't any on Earth either. They were a thing of the past. Modern devices made tattoos self-applicable, and anyone could apply them at home.

She had never indulged herself. Neither had her uncles. Her friend Inny had spent a couple of weeks playing around with it but in the end, reverted her skin to its natural pale coloring.

Ruby never had any interest. Not that she was ever overly concerned with outward appearance in that way. It was more that she simply didn't think they would look very good on her.

But she was here to fix a functional tattoo. That was different.

Looking around the room, it didn't seem too dissimilar from what she had seen in movies. They were clearly in a waiting area—but one with no chairs.

Artwork covered the walls, and that was one familiar feature: The artist displaying their abilities. Although, instead of flowers and skulls and other eclectic icons from human culture, most of what were on the walls here were little more than blobs. At least to her visual sensibilities. Colored blobs.

She walked up to one. It was a blue blob. Maybe not a blob, but a blue oval, with the right side of the oval a little thicker than the left. To the right of that, was a similar blue oval, but the thicker part was even thicker. To the right, the pattern continued. The shape morphed a few more times until five or six shapes later, what was a blue oval had morphed into a shape resembling a torus, one end of the oval wrapping around the other.

Ruby turned around and on the other side of the room was an entrance that led into another room. There was no door, so Ruby and the others could see in.

She saw Quiet Painter back there. Quiet Painter had three

chassis sections, like most robots in this Sector. But on what must be a daily basis, he changed his artwork. On one day, he would be the most tattooed robot she'd met, and on another, he was as bare as AT was. It only now struck her as potentially a little odd. Like, wouldn't he want to show off his wares more consistently?

Today, he was almost the least decorated robot in the room. Disto, who was generally the least tattooed robot she knew, was only slightly more decorated. And AT, was bare. But poking out of his chassis, Ruby could see Quiet Painter's multiple appendages that allowed him to execute his craft.

Right now, three of those appendages were active on another robot. The other robot was not one that Ruby recognized, which wasn't surprising. There were nearly 100 million robots on this planet. It wasn't like she was going to know each and every robot. There were almost five million in this Sector alone, according to what she had learned.

But this robot looked like it wasn't from around this Sector.

Not in the way that AT was obviously not from this Sector. The differences were more subtle. Like the form of the chassis... while SD and Disto and even Quiet Painter had chassis sections that all resembled squashed spheres, each of the three sections that made up this robot were more like if you took a cube, rounded the corners, and then squashed it.

She wasn't sure if she should be watching Quiet Painter work on this robot, but there was no door or other way to block the view.

Ruby turned around, but not before absorbing the seriously disturbing detail of what was getting airbrushed onto this robot: a family of humanoids. Not humans, but humanoids.

This caused Ruby to turn around more abruptly than she had planned, making a '*yip!*' noise in the process.

Disto rolled over. "I don't know that word."

"It wasn't a word, it was," Ruby waved both her hands in a way that was meant to help her brain conjure up an *actual* word, but it didn't work. She dropped her hands in defeat, "I don't know what that was."

Before Disto could ask anything else, Quiet Painter was escorting the other robot out of its studio. Quietly. He approached Ruby, Disto, and AT.

"I…" he started to say. Ruby leaned in closer. "What?"

"I do not…" Quiet Painter was certainly saying something. Ruby couldn't hear it.

"He said he doesn't work on robots of my design," AT offered. Disto was producing a slight nod to indicate he heard and agreed.

"Why not?" Ruby asked.

"Yes," Disto asked, "why not? That is unexpected…"

Ruby could hear Quiet Painter making some noise but again, it wasn't at a volume she could parse.

"Ah," Disto said. "It's his soft surface covering. Quiet Painter simply isn't equipped with the right kind of ink for that surface. He would be more than willing to submit a procurement request."

"But that's not why we're here," Ruby offered.

Quiet Painter perked up.

"My tattoos are fading," Ruby said. She took off her communicuff, and Disto offered to hold it. She held out her arms, undersides of the wrists pointed up.

Quiet Painter examined them and produced several beeps and chirps.

Disto translated, "He said that you're in luck that he happens to still have the proper ink for your version of a soft surface. That procurement request had been submitted at the time SD's mission began to find a Bio sample."

Ruby nodded, and Quiet Painter gestured with an appendage that she should follow him into the other room.

Disto and AT followed them. Ruby took in the entirety of the room, hoping to find a chair hiding in the corner. No such luck.

There were, however, three active screens on the wall, each showing a unique news channel.

"Um," Ruby began, "Are they going to, uh, line up exactly?" She looked at Disto as she said this and could read from his expression that he understood what she meant.

One of the tattoos was irrelevant. But the other, in combination with a tiny freckle on her wrist, gave her special access to the computer system of this world. Access that allowed her to help her robot friends and navigate the files of the 88.

Disto and Quiet Painter exchanged a few quick tones, most of which were barely audible to Ruby, and then Disto said, "Yes, there's still enough there that Quiet Painter can use to line up the tattoo. However, he cautioned us that there's *barely* enough. Next time, we need to come in earlier."

Ruby nodded, but hopefully a month into the future, she'd be back home and wouldn't have need of these tattoos. They'd be faded on her arm, a relic of her time here.

Unless she came back.

Was that likely? Or even possible? Going home and then returning? Or once they were able to send her home... that was it for her here. It was all simply over. And the memories would fade, and her questions wouldn't be answered, and over time it would all start to feel like one big dream.

She didn't get too far down that line of thought before she heard what could only be described as a gasp, simultaneously, from all three robots. Quiet Painter hadn't even started painting. He held her wrist and stared. But he wasn't staring at the wrist or at her.

All three robots were staring at the screens on the wall.

"What's going on?" Ruby said.

For a moment, no one answered.

"Disto, you're creeping me out. What's going on?"

"Shhh," Disto said.

The robots in the room were all deeply engrossed in watching the robot on the screen. Symbols flitted down the side of the screen while the robot produced several tones, beeps, and other sounds. It all sounded... somber.

After a minute or two, the robots came out of their trance, but Ruby could sense an unease, or a sadness or maybe it was anguish. Like they all had adorable puppies stolen from them.

AT made a noise and said, "The Hall of Templates put out an announcement. Several robot lines will be discontinued."

"Yes, occasionally, a line is discontinued. But never in the history that I'm familiar with have they discontinued so many at one time..." said Disto.

"Are," Ruby was a little nervous about asking this next question, "are any of you going to be, uh, discontinued?"

"No," Disto said.

Ruby let out the breath she didn't know she was holding.

"Well, that's something, I guess?"

"Indeed, but there are so many..."

"It must be a mistake," AT added.

"Who is going to be discontinued?" Ruby asked

Disto answered: "The lines that they announced will be discontinued were: Maniacal Manager; Honest Editor; Diplomatic Zookeeper; Frisky Scavenger; Slimy Scrubber; Offensive Escalator; Insecure Planner; and Stubborn Designer." He took a moment then added, "And they said there could be a second announcement coming soon."

"I've never heard of Offensive Escalator," AT said.

"It must be Sectorial," Disto said. "And be glad. They are quite unpleasant to talk to."

"But discontinued means that no new ones will be created, right?" Ruby asked.

Chapter 16

> Ambitious Technician <

"Correct," said AT. "However, discontinued lines are no longer supported. They don't receive updates and are not prioritized for maintenance. Discontinued robots fall into disrepair..."

AT trailed off, possibly stuck in a memory loop. He remembered when another robot, Costumed Barrier 17, of a short-lived line, had begged him to perform some maintenance. He couldn't, even if he wanted to, and he did. Want to, that was. But the tools he needed were no longer accessible.

Discontinued robots were given a number of tics until they were required to report to a recycling center. One could apply for an exemption through the lowest sub-node of the Reclamation and Recycling Division of the Agency of Resource Allocations, but AT was not aware that any had ever been granted.

No one spoke for several minutes, and AT was wondering if he should do anything special with these old memories of his. He was dwelling on them and that made his circuits uncomfortable.

"Well," he heard Ruby say to the room, "let's get this over with so we can figure out what to do."

He watched Quiet Painter carefully take the human's wrists

in his appendages. He began to tattoo.

AT watched Disto watch Ruby and Quiet Painter. This robot was obviously attached to Ruby. He felt... Jealous? That could be the word. AT wasn't always attuned to his feelings because they weren't always necessary.

Feelings were useful for many things. Retaining memories was aided when emotions were attached to them, getting a sense of trust based on the emotion someone may evoke, or being afraid or sad protecting oneself from going towards danger.

AT could imagine why jealousy may be necessary as well. Wanting something that you don't have—something that may fundamentally better your life—this motivation was useful in retrieving the said betterment.

Still, AT couldn't tell if this exact feeling of jealousy was necessary, though this didn't stop him from feeling it.

Disto was still holding the covering that Ruby handed him a few minutes ago.

"What is that?" He asked in a low tone so he wouldn't disturb Quiet Painter while he worked.

Disto looked in the direction that AT had pointed to, which happened to be its appendage, and said, "Ah, this curious device. This is Ruby's 'co-mune-ee-cuff' is what she calls it."

"She shed it?"

"Yes, it is not a part of her, similar to those outer garments she wears. They are on top of her chassis. Most bios have something similar. Not all, but most."

"Does it have a purpose?" AT asked.

"Oh my, yes! This is a fascinating device. Have you ever met a Fine Calculator?"

"Yes, once. It was several million tics ago."

"What about a Gentle Recorder? A Cowardly Correspondent?"

"Yes and no. How is this relevant?" AT was indeed confused by Disto's line of questioning.

"Well, this is going to push the limits of your imagination processor but try this thought experiment: Imagine you took a robot from all three of those lines and other lines and *combined* them."

AT did try to process that concept in his imagination. He brought to the surface of his processor an image of each of the robots Disto mentioned. While he never met a Cowardly Correspondent, he knew what they looked like since they were on the news channels all the time. He lined them up, side by side in his imagination, and then... combined them.

He imagined each of them with all of their various appendages extended and touching. But how were they touching? There were so many possibilities. Side by side? What about one on top of the other?

Each way AT tried to picture it, none of them came close to replicating a device small enough to wrap around the human's arm.

"I'm sorry, Disto. If I imagine three robots combined, I get a larger robot, not a smaller one."

Disto chuckled. "I'm sorry, I should have been more specific. Don't picture their bodies combined. Picture their circuits. Their algorithms."

That was a distinctly contrasting mental image and AT was not sure it was one he could grasp either.

He was starting to worry that Disto was going to think he was simple in the circuits.

Disto offered, "Or how's this... imagine a robot that could do all the things that all three of those robots could do. But also, do more."

AT found he could imagine that. Although he was still confused as to the form factor that this robot took. But before he could ask more, Disto was holding it up in an awkward way near his visual sensor.

"Pippa, meet Ambitious Technician, also known as AT."

"Hello," a voice said from the device.

"Greetings! Hello!" AT replied, shocked. "There is someone in there! May I hold it?"

"Yes," Disto said and handed it over, "Ah, it looks like Quiet Painter is finished."

"What are you?" AT asked as they moved back to Ruby's side.

"I am algorithm 51AI. A voice-controlled personal assistant, with personality and intelligence built-in."

"You are fascinating," AT remarked.

"Disto used the same word. And so did Scout."

"Who's Scout?" AT asked but didn't get an answer. Ruby grabbed Pippa from AT and said, "Thanks for holding this," and reattached it to her appendage.

"I tested the tattoo, and it worked," she declared. "So, we can get back to business."

AT was trying to parse what Ruby said. They had not previously been engaged in business, but rather an important discussion about the quality of the data held in the Hall of Templates. They were discussing how it could be fixed and the key AT possessed.

"Yes," Disto said, seeming undisturbed by Ruby's words. Disto turned to AT, "Now about that key…"

AT nodded, "I think it can help reconstruct some of the data."

"A key implies some kind of encoding or encryption. It sounds like there might have been encryption on top of an EPADAC algorithm in the past," Ruby said.

"EPADAC?" AT asked.

"Sorry. We acronymize everything. It stands for Error Prevention and Detection and Correction. It's exactly like it sounds… an algorithm that attempts to prevent errors, and when it can't prevent them, it tries to detect them, and when it detects them, it corrects them."

"Fascinating," AT said. Disto said nothing but had the look of a robot deep in thought. AT continued and questioned, "This is common among your people?"

"Oh yes, but I doubt most people know about it. Most people don't know how the technology they use works. But it's been around for ages. Our computer hardware is subject to errors mostly due to radiation coming from space."

AT couldn't suppress an involuntary noise his chassis made.

It caused his whole soft body to jiggle, also involuntarily.

"Are you... laughing?" Ruby asked.

AT didn't instantly recognize the Bio's word, 'laughing,' but once he looked it up, he attempted to shake his head to indicate that's indeed what he was doing.

After a few moments, he managed to control himself enough to speak again.

"Sorry, but when you said how most Bios do not know how things work... well, I could have said the same thing about most robots. But what was that other thing you mentioned. You said, 'radiation from space?'"

Ruby turned her head to the side but kept her ocular sensor trained on him. "Yeah, like the cosmic background radiation?"

"Disto, do you know about this?" AT said and nudged his chassis.

"Excuse me? I'm sorry—I was chasing my thought patterns through my circuits, I'm afraid."

"Do you know of radiation that is harmful to robots?" AT asked.

Disto shook his head. Both robots looked to Ruby for an explanation.

"Well, I only know a little. There are high-energy particles flying around in outer space in all directions. When they interact with other matter, they can kick off neutrons which can interfere with..." Ruby trailed off, crossed her arms and said gently, "and neither of you have any idea what I'm talking about."

Both robots now shook their heads.

Ruby sighed. "Okay, it's not important because who knows what's causing the errors in your systems. Maybe it's that, maybe it's something else. Either way, I can write you a new EPADAC algorithm that can work on new data that hasn't already been corrupted, but I think it's just as important that we are able to reconstruct or detect and correct the errors that are already present. And then, for real, I go home!"

"Agreed," AT and Disto said in unison.

Chapter 17

> Ruby <

Ruby sent all the robots away. She needed alone time with her MoDaC. And Pippa.

Ruby hadn't coded anything since she developed a compression and decompression algorithm for the robots. She helped them refine it a little after the initial release, but she hadn't touched it or any other code since.

That wasn't unusual. Coding was an activity she did as she needed or wanted to. It wasn't her whole life. Coding was a tool to get things done. When something didn't work, if a screwdriver couldn't fix it, most likely a piece of code could, and that's where she came in.

Ruby sighed, "Pippa, we're going to have to write our own EPADAC algorithm. From scratch."

Pippa didn't respond.

"Pippa?"

"We have to talk," the communicuff said.

"Are you breaking up with me?" Ruby said, smiling.

"What? I am not breaking anything…"

"Sorry, it was sort of a joke. I guess not a good one. Or wrong audience. Whatever you want to talk about, make it quick. We have a lot of work to do."

There was silence from Pippa once more.

"Pippa? Are you ready to help me write that EPADAC

algorithm?"

Once more, there was silence.

"Pippa?"

A new sigh emanated from the communicuff.

"You're the programmer, Ruby, not I."

That was true. Her communicuff's AI was... something else. AI did not program AI, did they? Was that built into their nature? As in, were the AIs from home built to not self-replicate or want to expand upon themselves and their functionality?

"Is that why robots haven't actually taken over yet?" Ruby muttered to herself.

Pippa was clearly puzzled, "I'm not sure I—"

"Don't worry about it."

Ruby wanted to know more about who and how they were programmed, but it would have to wait until she was back home. Pippa's code was locked up tight.

And that was not important right now.

"Agreed. I am the programmer. But... will you be my test engineer?"

"Please explain."

"Well, what I write needs to be tested. And we usually write the tests first. So, we have a roadmap, so we know what the code is supposed to do. The tests drive the development. Does that make sense, Pippa?"

There was a pause. Pippa then said, "Yes, I understand. But isn't that a form of programming as well?"

Ruby paused and tried to recall the last time she participated in tests of any kind. She had skipped testing when she wrote the compression algorithm—because she was still freaking out over being on an alien world—and the result was that she forgot to initially include decompression.

She still cringed at the image of Honest Editor freaking out when he didn't know what to do with his compressed data. Especially since that was her fault and could have been avoided if she'd been more careful.

Testing was always the first thing to be brushed aside when

under a tight schedule. Everyone knew that. Everyone knew how bad that was. Yet, it was still common, and here Ruby was, living proof that it still happened.

But not this time.

"Well, yes, but there are two, uh, I'll call them 'levels.' There's a first level where we plan out the tests and the second level where we make them. Would you be more comfortable planning out the tests, Pippa?"

Again, a pause that was a smidge longer than it should be. Enough so that Ruby repeated, "Pippa?"

"I can try, but without a connection to the networks I'm expected to have, I have access to fewer resources and my knowledge is limited. I may need additional input from you."

Ruby pursed her lips together tightly. Crud. This was going to be like if she asked her seven-year-old cousin Sebastian to take on this task. Pippa was utterly unprepared, utterly untrained, and probably had no idea where to even begin.

"Okay, well, maybe start by finding some data I can use as a test case?" Ruby offered.

"Like the corrupted star chart?"

"Well, sort of. I can't uncorrupt that data until I know the algorithm is working. I need something that we can deliberately introduce an error into and then check the results of processing it through the algorithm back with the original.

"So, yeah, we could use the star chart, but only if we change more of its information. Honestly, it would be less confusing if we used something else."

"I understand. I will find some data, Ruby."

"Good. And I'll get to work writing this algorithm. I wonder if I can deconstruct an algorithm already in use by my MoDaC…"

Ruby trailed off, face engrossed in her MoDaC, and lit up with a slight blue hue from the light it gave off.

Chapter 18

> Austere Agent <

Austere Agent was not happy. He was not meant for data entry and manipulation work. His algorithms supported observation and investigation. He sat in front of an access terminal in the Agency of Templates, radiating unhappiness. None of the other agents at their access terminals were necessarily radiating anything else. Agents typically wanted to be out and about, not handling data entry.

But ever since the Hysterical Analyst line had been discontinued, more of that data manipulation work fell directly to agents.

And since he was the one who told Detailed Historian to file the interface request, his unique identifier was on it, so it was routed back to him for initial processing.

He reviewed the information. He was looking for an easy way to deny the request. If they had missed any bit of information that was required per the instructions under Directive 11, he could do so, and no one would question the integrity of the situation.

Of course, Detailed Historian and his Bio friend could appeal, but he didn't need to worry about that now.

Directive 11 was the master set of instructions for all interfaces. It was a long and lengthy set, covering all the details of every known interface and what to do in the case of an unknown interface as presented itself.

All the standard details were included. Full identifier of the requester with contact details. "Detailed Historian N" That was interesting. It was rare for a robot to have no numerical identifier as part of his full information. It happened, but it was rare.

And it was not sufficient reason for denying the request.

Austere Agent moved on to the section that described the two sides of the interface requested to be made. There was a section on whether or not the details of the second side were known. Austere Agent was expecting that 'unknown' would have been selected and was mildly surprised when it was not.

The Bio must have provided details on the expected interface from her system.

The details were regarding how the interface would occur. Similar to how Swell Driver interfaced with the Bio initially, they were asked to allow Swell Driver to knowingly accept another ship.

That brought up some interesting questions for Austere Agent. Did Swell Driver have the right approvals to do this in the first place?

Austere Agent was already logged into his computer console. That was how he was reviewing this request, after all.

He paused. He knew he needed to look up the available information on Swell Driver's journey to how and why he found the Bio, but he didn't want to. The system had been slow all day. Access requests into the The Core's main memory were slow. He put in the request for information anyway.

While he was waiting for a response, he turned his circuits to the other task at hand. This ridiculous idea of a wireless communications interface Prodigal Agent had spoken about. It was a nice idea. It would likely be faster than what he was dealing with right now.

He recalled the information on the wireless interface request from his local memory. He, as did most other Agents, took the Bio's compression algorithm. While it was incompatible with a few robots, those were all rare and unusual circumstances.

In his case, Austere Agent was glad he did it, so he could have additional data available at all times.

Prodigal Agent transferred all the information he had on the wireless interface. The form used for the request that Prodigal approved wasn't too different from what he had now.

The most interesting piece of that was the identifier: Invisible Scout. Austere Agent looked up Invisible Scout in Location Zero Access List. There was no such robot.

Austere Agent made an audible chirp. The other robots at other access points here in the Agency of Interfaces main office all turned to face him.

"Excuse me," he said. They all turned back to their respective tasks.

He double checked. No, no Invisible Scout. Putting that detail aside for a moment, he turned his attention to the details of the interface request itself. It was indeed the specifications for a wireless communication. He wasn't sure he even knew how he knew since he had never seen such a thing before. Had he? No, he had not, according to a quick scan of the local archive he kept that was a list of interfaces he had personally worked on.

But there it was. In glorious detail.

The instruction that Prodigal Agent had provided was that Austere Agent should get to the root of this request. With no way to contact the originator, the next best thing would be to attempt to implement the interface to see if it was real or not. Yes, that was the right thing to do. First, he would need to find the right equipment or have himself modified.

Before he could finish drafting a detailed implementation plan, the console in front of him lit up with the information he had originally requested.

He scanned it and was surprised at what he learned. Apparently, when the various Driver line robots are on missions far from Location Zero, they have a wide latitude to do anything they need to get the job done. Such were the directions from the Special Project associated with Swell

Driver's trip. Intriguing. Especially since Austere Agent curiously received more information than he requested.

Apparently, Swell Driver had been going on other trips recently but not directed by the Special Project that sent him to Ruby Palmer's home. In this case, information was limited. Surprisingly limited. So little information was available, in fact, that no robot could have possibly made an informed decision to approve this.

That was interesting and Austere Agent would bookmark that to study later. Right now, he was more interested in the task regarding the wireless communication interface.

He approved Detailed Historian's request and left the Agency's office to go in search of some equipment.

> Swell Driver <

"Goodbye, Swell Driver. May your existence be protracted and conclusive."

Swell Driver stood at the entrance to Rejuvenation Region 1010. He did indeed feel rejuvenated to an extent. At least, he had an alternate feeling, one that was closer to what he remembered normal to be like.

He looked at his new friend and counselor, Explosive Healer, who had concluded her farewell.

"Thank you, Healer," SD said. "I wish you well on your journey of observation."

Explosive Healer nodded, slowly turned around, and started moving back towards the innards of the region, stopping to visually examine a spot on the floor before continuing in.

Yes, SD did indeed feel rejuvenated. But more importantly, he had managed to protect his data. His star chart. The one that Ruby needed. The one that he would use to help her get home. Even though she took a copy, Ruby had explained that right now, all the data on the planet was at risk of getting corrupted. He was certain that his was not. He didn't know how he knew it—he simply knew.

SD reviewed a list he had created earlier. It was one of the suggested coping strategies. He had always been able to make lists, but Explosive Healer broke down the concept of the list in detail.

"You will take comfort in representing abstract data as a countable number of ordered values," Explosive Healer had said in one of the group sessions.

A robot SD never learned the name of, who was quite jittery, said, "but… but if something is on the list more than once?"

"That's okay," Healer said in a reassuring voice. "Duplicates can be removed.

"A list is a container, nothing more. It's one of the tools you were gifted when you were created, but it's one of several tools that we're not taught how to use properly.

"Lists are calming. They are calming because they are finite. Finite things bring order and calm to the universe.

"And be thankful that all of you are of the modern era… there were robots in the past that didn't have lists and all the operations built in. It was a time of greater chaos."

He constructed a new empty list and called it 'To Execute.' He made sure it was empty, then he added the first item to it: 'Find Ruby.'

Executing that first item wouldn't be too difficult. The next item was 'Take Ruby home.' SD knew he had the means to do this. In fact, he might be the only one who could do this. He possessed potentially the only uncorrupted star map from when he traveled to her solar system originally. But more than that, he retained a memory of that trip. He could correlate that memory record to the map—that's how he knew his map was good.

In fact, he paused to create a second list to address the star map. He needed to protect it and made sure that second list was linked to the first.

Finally, the last thing on his list was the one he wanted to think about least, but it had to be there: 'Purge unpleasant thoughts.' He knew there were multiple algorithms inside of him that shouldn't be there, and he also knew that if he ruminated on them too much, it would be problematic, but he didn't know what problems they would cause. He wanted to get rid of them.

Without telling Explosive Healer or anyone else in the Region, SD managed to come away with some coping mechanisms. He wanted to tell Healer, but couldn't bring himself to say the words out loud: "There are voices in my head."

No matter how gentle, caring, coping, or otherwise they were in the Rejuvenation Region, mentioning a problem like that was surely guaranteed to get him back into reprogramming.

Instead, SD made one final list to address this item which he labeled, 'Find the Others.' He didn't know if he meant 'Others' as a label for those voices, or 'Others' as something separate from himself. When he invoked the word 'Others,' the word 'enigma' involuntarily formed in his circuits. Certainly, there must be a connection. He needed to figure this out, possibly find out who or what the Others were. But first, he needed to take care of his friend, Ruby.

Chapter 19

> Ruby <

"Based on what you've told me about the Core," Ruby began, "We can't do this like last time. Security has been tightened."

"This needs to be more of a digital campaign effort... analogous to how we pass around the 88 algorithm," Disto offered.

"Perhaps we initiate a new one," added AT.

"Start a new chain?" Ruby offered. "The way you explained it to me, it's similar to what *we* call a chain. I only know a little about how they work. Back home, that's a religious programming sect. Not something I was allowed to explore..."

Ruby and her robot friends were slowly making their way through the Museum of Intricate Specimens. This was Ruby's second visit to the Museum. Her first visit was on her initial tour of the Sector. It was Disto's suggestion to return since new items had been installed, and it would look suspicious if they were all hanging out at any of their enclaves too much, and other public places were too public.

There were not many other robots in the Museum. It was not a place frequented by many at any given time, so it was the least suspicious place they could be.

Ruby found the place strange and unorganized. Museums were supposed to have themes. History. Technology. Bad Art. Dog Collars. Yes, she knew there was a Dog Collar Museum someplace on Earth, but she had never been. Of course, living on a space station most of her life meant she had never been to most places she'd heard or read about on Earth. Maybe she'd make a point to visit all the obscure museums when she got back. If she ever did get back.

But here in this museum—she applied the term 'museum' loosely in her head—it was more like: Collection of random things that have nothing to do with each other that someone didn't want to throw away. Nothing here was particularly intricate or 'fancy' as Disto had once tried to describe the items.

The group stood in front of a raised pedestal that came up to her waist.

One thing Ruby did acknowledge: This smelled like what she imagined a museum might smell like.

Astroll 2 contained a narrow and cramped museum that was all about the history of asteroid mining. But it was so small, only two people could fit in there at once. Even that was a lot of space to waste on a *museum*, some argued.

She had been in that constricted space a few times. As part of her education, Ruby was required to learn the history, plus, she did find the history of asteroid mining interesting.

In particular, she enjoyed learning about the brave explorers, navigating the dangerous asteroid belt, mining the tumbling rocks for minerals that were either depleted or too difficult to mine on Earth.

The object on this pedestal, however, looked like it was a tool of some sort. Ruby couldn't make it out, nor could she read most of the symbols on the small placard below. She cringed as she considered asking Disto or one of the others to translate. She was trying to rely on them less for simple tasks—it was like she was using them as a tool each time she did.

Instead, she leaned in a little closer until she lost her balance. It happened so quickly. Her arms flailed out and before one of them struck the pedestal, AT had his soft arms out and caught her.

"Oh sheesh," she said, half startled. The pedestal remained

untouched and where it was. "Thank you, AT. I don't know what happened. I'm normally not that clumsy, I promise."

Back on her feet, she was ready to ignore the artifacts and focus on the task at hand.

"It will take longer," said Disto. "In addition, this needs to be implemented where all the data is… it's not only us as individual robots, but the Core, the whole structure. Every single robot and every repository of information needs to be a node in algorithm."

"Excuse me, but you sound more like an Essential Guru rather than a Detailed Historian," AT said, adding, "Not that I've ever met any robot of any Historian line before."

"Essential Guru? That's a robot line?" Ruby asked. That didn't entirely fit with her idea of all the robot lines. Gurus were… spiritual leaders.

Disto produced his version of a chuckle.

"Yes," Disto answered, adding, "I have not met a Guru, but I am aware of them. They…," he paused, "They are the people who develop," he waved an appendage, "requirements."

Ruby understood. She knew exactly what requirements were, but they were things left to the domain of marketing engineers. There were two on the station, friends of her uncles, and she remembered them chuckling one day on how they were neither in marketing, nor engineers. And according to Uncle Logan—an engineer of sorts and employed on the station as an odorist, he received requirements from these individuals, and knew they were almost always wrong. Or so she'd heard or been told. She had no first-hand experience except as a school project beyond the offhand comments from her uncles.

"I understand. We're going to figure out what the requirements are before we implement this algorithm," Ruby offered.

"Precisely," Disto and AT said in unison.

"Have either of you done this before?" Ruby asked.

"Not exactly," said AT. "I have reviewed several sets of requirements as part of various systems I needed to repair to help understand the expected functional state."

AT turned expressionless as he delved into several memories. "Unambiguous, short, feasible, prioritized, testable, consistent, and singular. Those are the requirements for requirements. I am supposed to flag any set of requirements I come across that do not meet these criteria as invalid."

That list of criteria sounded completely logical to Ruby. It sounded perfect. It sounded pretty easy.

"Ok, who is taking notes? Let's get this done!"

Disto moved over to the console and logged in to indicate he would be the note taker. Ruby was relieved. As the only human, the only Bio, she was worried they'd make her do it. She'd probably be the least efficient of them in doing so.

"First," Disto said, "Each robot and each system that uses the algorithm is a node."

"Problem," AT said. "That's not singular."

"Each robot that uses the algorithm is a node. Each system that uses the algorithm is a node. Is that acceptable?" asked Disto.

"Why can't you combine them?" Ruby offered. "For this purpose, wouldn't a robot be considered a system? So don't you simply need 'each system that uses the algorithm is a node.'"

AT produced a new snorting noise, "I agree with Ruby."

Disto noted that. "Recorded. What is next?"

"Here are the next few: Each node has a ledger. The initial ledger given to every node is identical. Each piece added to the algorithm is communicated to every node. Any node receiving a new piece performs a check. If the check is a successful validation, that information, to include the verification logic is provided to every other node. Every receiving node performs the validation and updates their ledger."

"Pippa, are you listening in?"

"Yes, of course."

"Open a new note. I don't have my MoDaC, so I'm going to dictate. I want to stare at this and contemplate it later. Call the note requirements criteria. Contents of the note:

Unambiguous, short, feasible, prioritized, testable, consistent, and singular."

Ruby paused to gather her thoughts. *These requirements were short. But they were far from unambiguous. In fact, they were all very ambiguous. Emphasis on 'big'.*

"Is that all?" Pippa asked.

"Yeah, but maybe take some notes from the conversation."

"I can record the whole thing if you'd like."

Ruby nodded. She turned back to Disto.

"Ok, for the sake of argument, let's assume this is all we need. How do we get the ledger into the Core and all the nodes that must make up the Core? Specifically, your Hall of Templates?"

AT and Disto pondered the question as much as they pondered the museum pieces in front of them.

The two of them came to stop in front of a shadowbox on the wall. Inside the box, Ruby saw what looked like a remote with a single button mounted in the center. She wasn't sure if it was a remote, or something else, or if it held any meaning or significance to the two robots who were staring at it.

They weren't making any noise, but they were looking at each other as if they were communicating remotely, which Ruby knew couldn't be the case. Maybe they were thinking the same thing?

"I calculate the odds in our favor at 321 to 1 if we encourage an amalgamation of robots to appear at the same time at the Hall of Templates," Disto said.

"I calculate the odds a little less at 297 to 1. But I suspect that is because I am not as familiar with the local robots," AT offered.

"Are you suggesting we storm the gates?" Ruby asked.

Disto and AT exchanged another look, "I believe that is an accurate analogy," said Disto.

"We need to put out a message for all willing robots to meet us at the entrance to the Hall at a time of our choosing."

"What time?" asked Ruby.

"Well, how long until you finish your algorithm?"

"Ah—that… it's written, but it's not fully tested." Ruby glared at her communicuff. She knew Pippa could see her face, even if its avatar wasn't actively hovering.

"What if we did a live test as well?"

"On Swell Driver?" Ruby asked.

"Precisely what I was thinking, Ruby," Disto said. "We need to locate him first."

Chapter 20

> Fearless Communicator <

It was so obvious, but he didn't see the answer until now. After all, he was a communicator, and his programming was quite limited when it came to things that were not communication. Like space travel. He didn't know that much about spaceships or how they worked or what it was like to be traveling through space.

Fearless Communicator had never been on a spaceship after all. He had never left his homeworld. Most robots rarely did. Only robots like those of Swell Driver's lineage and the various Explorer lineages. He was certain there had at one time even been a Prospector lineage.

But Communicators? He didn't know the history of his line, but he was certain that they didn't go anywhere. Or did they?

It wasn't relevant.

What was relevant is that the answer was so simple, it was so obvious.

They should send a ship to message back to Ruby's homeworld. Not broadcast a message but send a ship that could carry it.

They could send Ruby, too, but she was here. She wouldn't be sent until she went home—which was the opposite purpose of sending a message.

But a ship. A small delivery ship. In fact, they were a line of robots all their own. Trifling Probe was the line. FC couldn't remember when he first heard of them. It must have been on the news broadcast.

FC was logged into a console, as was typical for him. He was rarely *not* logged in.

He looked up information about the probes. They were tiny. A third of the size of his own top chassis. That was small.

FC put in a requisition request to use one.

While he was waiting for a response, he sent a message to Ruby to let her know that she should record a message and that he found a way to deliver it in a matter of tens of tics rather than thousands or millions of them.

Ruby's response came first. She was thrilled and excited and used some other words he needed to add to his vocabulary on her native language. She said she'd record a message shortly.

It wasn't long after that FC also received a response to his requisition request.

"1000 Trifling Probes are prepared for departure. Awaiting instructions."

FC paused. He re-examined his request. He did indeed ask for one. How he was getting 1000 was a little confusing.

FC considered that. Maybe this was a good thing. Redundancy. Yes, redundancy. Each Probe would carry the message, and they would provide full communication coverage in Ruby's home system. After all, he wasn't sure *exactly* where within her system to send it. This would ensure that her message was wide reaching, and the right people would get it.

This was going to work out perfectly.

Chapter 21

> Ruby <

Disto had returned to his enclave to see if he could track down SD. He wanted to log in with the privacy only offered by his enclave. Ruby suspected there was more to that but didn't press the issue.

Ruby and AT were on their way to the Hall of Templates. Their current task was to simply walk by and scout out the current scene there.

Ruby had taken off her communicuff and was doing her best to watch where she was walking while examining it.

"What are you doing?" AT asked.

"I'll tell you later," she responded.

Ruby knew that Pippa or some piece of the communicuff was always active and could record anything she said. It had to. There was no other way for it to come alive when she said 'Pippa' if it wasn't listening all the time.

Ruby was looking for a way to turn it off. Recent interactions with the AI made her slightly uncomfortable, and she wanted to know if she could turn it off or at least mute the microphone, so she could have a private conversation.

She was definitely not going to ask Pippa directly for instructions on how to do this, because that would alert Pippa to her discomfort and that was a level of uncomfortableness she was not slightly, but intensely, uncomfortable with.

Then she realized…

"AT, we need to stop back at my quarters."

AT nodded and implied that Ruby lead the way. Ruby was now quite familiar with the local area on this level and exuded confidence while navigating her way around from wherever they came from. Her directional sense wasn't fully tuned, but it was good enough.

She took a wrong turn and had to double back only half the time. Not a big deal—it meant it took her a little longer.

This time, however, they made it back to her quarters in record time.

Since her tattoo was working perfectly, she opened the door without issue and placed the communicuff onto the table.

"I'll be back shortly," she said to it and walked back to the hallway where AT was waiting.

With the door closed behind her, Ruby felt lighter. She hadn't been without her communicuff like this since her first few days at Location Zero. She liked Pippa, but Pippa was *off* in a way she couldn't explain.

AT was obviously waiting for an explanation.

"I wanted to be able to talk without it listening," she stated. "I was looking for some kind of off switch, but I don't think it has one."

"I would love to know more about the device," AT said. "Perhaps I can examine it later?"

"Sure," Ruby said. "But just so you know, the AI in it doesn't always… I don't know. Something isn't right with it."

"AI?"

"Yeah, it stands for 'Artificial Intelligence.'"

"Artificial? How is it artificial?"

"It's human-made."

"'human-made'?"

"Yeah, like, humans created it, but not naturally, so it's artificial."

"What is the natural way for humans to create intelligence?"

Ruby considered how best to answer. She, of course, completely understood how humans procreated, and she had explained most of it to Disto the week before, but Disto stopped her from completing the overview, saying that he generally knew how Bios reproduced and that humans weren't terribly unique in that area, and it was too messy for him to think about.

But she also explained that that wasn't exactly how she was created, either. Her mom had some reproductive help with a doctor. As did her grandmother.

She was explaining all of this to AT, too, who stopped her in the middle and said, "Pause, please. You weren't created naturally, either?"

"Excuse me?"

"You said, and I quote, 'My mother underwent a procedure where DNA was selected and combined with hers,'" AT said. "That is not the same as the 'natural way' you described immediately before that. You were also created by artificial means. Does this not also label you as 'artificial intelligence'?"

Ruby didn't know what to say. That wasn't exactly what the term meant. AI was... not biological... right? Before she could think any longer, AT interrupted her thoughts, "And what does this make me? Us?"

"Well, you're robots."

"What is a robot?"

Wow, AT was making her think hard about things she hadn't thought before. And that's saying a lot because living on a space station, and piloting around does give one a lot of time to think.

"Well, you have an independent body, for one."

"Are all robots intelligent?"

"Not on my world, but they certainly are here."

"Are they?" AT looked around and pointed to some small robots flying through the hallway. He gestured toward them. "Are *they?*"

"I don't know what they are."

"They are micro sensors. They collect data and send it to the Agency that is responsible for them. The Agency of Type Checkers, the Agency of Process Improvement, and especially the Hall of Performance and Metrics—they all have micro sensors about. Nothing intelligent there. You can't even have a conversation with them. You can poll them for a few bits of data, but that's it. That's not terribly intelligent."

"No, it's not," Ruby was forced to concede.

"So, what makes an entity intelligent?"

Ruby didn't have an answer to that. *I think, therefore I am? Is that intelligence?*

"I thought there were Philosopher line robots that were supposed to have these conversations. You're just a..."

"Technician?" AT chuckled. "Well, yes. But that doesn't mean I can't ask these questions."

"But doesn't that mean you're doing something you weren't programmed to do?"

"No."

"But... I'm confused."

"It's simple. I am a problem solver. That means I am programmed to ask questions. Like why? Why is this broken? Well, this stopped doing what it was expected to do. Why did it stop doing that? Because it lost power. Why did it lose power?" AT paused presumably to make sure Ruby was listening. "You see, I have to ask questions so I can get to the root of the problem. Asking about intelligence is no different. We have a problem. We don't know something. That this is similar to what a philosopher does is entirely coincidental. In fact, I might suggest that I'd make a better Philosopher than any of the actual Philosophers."

Ruby smiled "I would agree."

"Good. We agree. So back to the original question. Why am I intelligent? Why is your device 'artificial' and you're 'natural' even though you both are intelligent? And please describe more about your mom. She is another human, yes? I would like to meet her."

Ruby's stomach turned into a block of iron, and the color drained from her face.

"You can't," she said.

"Oh. Is this conversation now making you uncomfortable,

Ruby?"

"Yes. Very."

And then a piercing noise emanated from all around and knocked her off her feet.

> Ambitious Technician <

"Are you well?" AT asked Ruby, who was no longer using her two long appendages to keep herself upright. They had gone limp, and the majority of her chassis was on the floor.

All the robots around them had stopped, too, as a result of the tone emanating throughout the hallways, which—after the initial five tics—had reduced in volume to a dull beat.

It was the same tone used in his home region, so he recognized it as a 'stop—there's an emergency nearby' order. He had stopped. No big deal. The Bio's reaction was more interesting.

"Wha…?" Ruby said. She held out one of her upper appendages. It took AT a moment to calculate that it was an indication to grab hold and help her back to her original position.

Once she was upright again with her face oriented toward his visual sensors, she used her top appendages to brush off the rest of her body. He wasn't sure what she was brushing off, he could see nothing on her besides the artificial coverings she wore. He tittered as one of his circuits tingled at the concept of 'artificial.'

He registered he was now going to titter each time he heard or even thought of the word 'artificial.' He briefly contemplated building a comedy routine out of it. As a hobby.

"There is a calamity in the nearby area," AT said. "But we are well."

"Speak for yourself. That was intense! What kind of 'calamity'?"

"Intense?"

"Yeah, didn't you hear it? I mean, that could have made my ears bleed."

"The strength of the warning was indeed high. But that's intentional since it's a warning. To ensure it gets everyone's attention."

"Yeah, I got that, but attention for *what?*"

The alarm was still active, but AT saw that Ruby was functional, so he maneuvered around the inert robots in the hallway to a kiosk. Once connected, he accessed the available data and images.

"Oh my," he said.

Ruby followed him, taking the exact same path around the robots he had, and was at his side. "What did you find out?" she said, but she wasn't looking at him, she was using her optical sensors to scan the scene around them.

With urgency, she said, "and does it have anything to do with that?" One of her upper appendages was pointed in the direction of a hallway perpendicular to the one they were in. Smoke was emanating from the hallway.

"Indeed! I think so," AT said. "Apparently, there has been an accident and it is around that corner."

He gathered all the data he could from the kiosk, then said, "Let's go. I think it involves someone you know."

AT logged out of the console—the worst thing he could do would be forget that action—and moved in the direction of the smoke at a brisk pace that wasn't too fast where he couldn't navigate around the other robots in the hallway.

Ruby was following him and shouted, "Someone I know? SD?"

"No," he said as he turned the corner. The hallway was a short entrance to the Inner Nonagon.

He stopped abruptly as he saw a mangle of robots, a kiosk, and what was now mostly unrecognizable equipment.

"One of the other robots made famous by your actions," AT said and pointed at the heap.

As Ruby caught up to him, she abruptly stopped her forward motion, put her appendages over her mouth, and a sound AT couldn't parse into words escaped Ruby's body.

Chapter 22

> Ruby <

Ruby gasped.

"Honest Editor!" she shouted. She recognized her friend in the rubble.

Barely.

Her mouth hung open as she took in the scene before her. It was a lump that appeared to be made up of a few robots—she couldn't tell exactly how many—and some pieces of equipment, maybe a kiosk—that must have been standing there minding its own business when a lump of robots crashed into it.

Everything within the lump was at an odd angle to each other. The only way Ruby recognized that there were other robots entangled in the mess were the various chassis bulbs that were flashing through colors in the way these robot chassis did.

Honest Editor's body was at the head of the pack, but its body was pushed in toward it, and his head was at an angle it should not have been, facing her.

Sparks popped here and there in the pile and the smoke appeared to be coming from the far end, against the equipment that was the immovable force that stopped the whole thing.

When Ruby looked up and away, she could see where the pack had come from through the park.

There were dozens of onlookers. AT was engaged in conversation with several of them in their native tones.

After a few moments, he addressed Ruby.

"They saw the whole thing. Honest Editor came in screaming... profanities, I'll call it... and grabbed a robot, pushed him into three more, and then the group became a fused mass picking up speed through the area. By that time, others could avoid getting caught up, and they drove around until crashing into this kiosk."

"I can't believe it! What would make Honest Editor do such a thing?"

"I don't know, Ruby, but I suggest we go. I don't like the uninformed conclusions others are drawing right now."

Ruby felt AT's soft appendage touch her. He was trying to nudge her away.

"But Honest Editor? We can't leave him like this?"

"Yes, we can. There will be robots who are equipped to handle an incident like this. You and I are not right now."

"But I want to stay to make sure he's alright," Ruby said and took a step closer to the pile.

As she did, she heard a collective noise come from the onlookers. They were all looking at her as much as they were looking at the wreckage in front of them.

As Ruby looked around, the robotic faces that were looking back at her had lost the previous friendliness they had.

"Okay, AT, let's go," she said.

As they made their way away from the wreckage and out of the park, Ruby could hear a cacophony of sounds pick up behind them.

AT was behind her and gently pushing her to go a little faster.

"He's going to be okay, though," Ruby said as they got into the hallway. The previous klaxon sound was now almost gone, and robots were moving freely again, although an unusual number of them were headed in the direction they came from to see the results of the accident for themselves.

When AT didn't answer right away, she stopped and turned

to face him and repeated herself, "he's going to be okay?"

Ruby didn't yet have a sense for how AT emoted, since the coloring scheme that she had come to get used to for the other robots wasn't as applicable with AT, but he wasn't answering with a resounding and confident 'why, yes!' and that worried her.

"I calculate that given that his line has been scheduled for discontinuation, resources won't be expended to return him to a functioning condition. I'm sorry."

Ruby didn't know what to say. Loss of friends... well, she had never had many friends to lose so she had never experienced this kind of loss. There was only the big loss of her mother, and that had been it.

She didn't know what to say or do or how to process this.

AT must not have known what to say or do with Ruby, so he stood there staring at her as much as she was staring at him.

It was awkward.

"Were you implying back there that those robots think I had something to do with this?"

"Let's keep moving and I'll tell you exactly what I heard," AT said and gestured for her to move.

She did move, one leg in front of the other, without the purpose or certainty of a destination. She walked aimlessly with a robot following her.

As they moved, AT told her that amongst the onlookers, they were speculating that Ruby's now famous compression algorithm caused this.

Honest Editor was the first one to process the algorithm, and adverse side effects were now showing themselves. He received the algorithm first, so he was showing the effects first.

This stopped Ruby in her tracks once more. "No..." she said. "They can't really believe that, can they? I helped everyone..."

"I know you did, and I've seen the algorithm. But you can't stop people from believing what is going to help them process an event such as this."

Ruby hadn't been paying attention to where they were

walking. It was a wandering... but they managed to wander right to Disto's enclave door.

> Ruby <

The door whooshed open before Ruby or AT touched anything.

Disto was standing there and ushered them both inside.

"Your timing is impeccable," Disto said.

Ruby sat herself down onto the floor since there were still no chairs in Disto's enclave. Last time she was here she kidded him about it. This time, she wasn't in any mood for joking around, so she sat on the ground and let the weight of the day keep her there. Gravity kept her there, too, noticeably so as she felt much heavier than normal.

"Don't get comfortable," Disto added. "We're going to get SD. And you have a message to send."

"I do?"

"Yes, you're going to record a message that we will insert into the news broadcasts to explain to all of robot-kind that you are not responsible for Editor's condition. You need to request that every able and willing robot needs to meet us."

Ruby's stomach sank. This was not the first broadcast she'd been asked to participate in. After her compression algorithm was deployed, she was on the news all the time. Those broadcasts were recorded and recreated into several short video snippets that were continuously used to convince the robots to accept the upgrade. Many of them featured a cheerful and content Honest Editor.

If robots could blush, Honest Editor would have been blushing as Ruby repeatedly mentioned how thankful she was that he was a brave robot who was willing to trust her.

Now it all seemed... well... *stupid*. Self-indulgent. Vain.

It all made her feel a little fake.

"Stand up, Ruby," Disto interrupted her thoughts. "Go to your quarters and record your message. AT should accompany you. I will meet you there with SD."

"SD? You know where he is?"

"Indeed... No time to explain. On your feet."

"Feet!" blurted AT. "Ah!"

Ruby saw that Disto ignored AT and that he was looking her over.

"Where is your communicuff?"

"Oh. I left it in my quarters. We just came from there."

"That's the first time I've seen you without it in a while."

Ruby wasn't certain this was the right moment to reveal that she didn't entirely trust Pippa. Disto had proved to be one of the most ultra-logical beings she'd ever met, yet for some reason she was worried that he would overreact.

Before she could respond, AT blurted out, "Those are called feet!" He was pointing at Ruby's feet as she untangled them from the cross-legged pose she had put herself in and stood up. "I didn't have a label for that part of your body. In fact, when we're done here, I want to make sure I have an accurate understanding of all your components."

Ruby walked out of Disto's quarters at a brisk pace. Followed by AT. Followed by Disto, who didn't seem to appreciate AT's interruption. She appreciated it thoroughly because she could conveniently ignore Disto's last question and repeat one of her own.

"Do you know where SD is?"

"I'll explain when we see you later." And with that, he took off in the opposite direction Ruby and AT were headed, faster than she'd ever seen Disto move. So fast, he almost knocked a robot out of the way.

She looked at AT. "Come on. Human anatomy lesson later, but I could probably label a few more parts while we're walking."

"I would appreciate that," said AT. "I am curious as to how far you decompose the nomenclature for your components and sub-components."

"Pretty far. Why are you interested?"

"I am a technician. I am preparing in case I have to make a repair."

"A repair? To…" Ruby put the pieces together in her mind. "To me?" She gestured at herself but tried to keep walking, keeping her eyes in front of her, so she didn't bump into anyone.

"Of course. You could be damaged as easily as anyone else, no?"

Ruby hadn't considered that. She didn't perceive what they were about to do as dangerous. They were simply programming computers. It was the least dangerous activity she knew of.

But AT had a point.

No doctors. No first aid. Medical technology had come so far for humans, but here, she didn't have access to any of it. Except that her communicuff would be loaded with a host of emergency medical information. Ruby grimaced as she acknowledged to herself that she probably should always have it with her at all times, for exactly this reason.

"Yeah, AT. I can be." she said. And was silent after that.

> Disto <

"Where is your communicuff?"

"Oh. I left it in my quarters. We just came from there."

Disto replayed that interaction of a few minutes ago over and over as he made his way down the hallway.

Up until then, Disto—quite deliberately—did not pass on all of the knowledge he had collected recently to Ruby. It wasn't about Ruby; it was that he had been certain that the walls in his own enclave couldn't be trusted.

At least, that was until he saw Ruby without her communicuff. She said she left it in her quarters. She said 'left' instead of a word like 'forgot.' Communication specifics mattered. Ruby's response was not what he would have predicted. His initial assumption was that she must have forgotten it, but she clearly knowingly left it there.

The communicuff was an interesting being in its own right, and leaving it alone in her quarters sounded… cruel. In his albeit brief interactions with the entity designated Pippa, he concluded that all it wanted was companionship—it didn't want to be left alone.

It was also a useful augmentation to Ruby's biological state. Bios had so many traits that were imprecise or imperfect. Like how their memory was fallible.

But Pippa, similar to any other robot, could recall things with perfect accuracy.

Except when there were errors. Disto didn't like to admit that he could have errors in his own memory, but that's what they were trying to correct.

Prevent, detect, and *correct,* he reminded himself.

Before they all left his enclave, Disto had wanted to talk to Ruby more about it, but there had been no time to ask Ruby about her auxiliary entity. That would have to wait.

Disto had been connected to his console and power source in record time and was flying through the system to locate SD. Ruby and AT were engaged in their own conversation and not paying much attention to him.

At least that was until he had blurted out a tone that he knew AT would recognize and didn't have a translation that Ruby would understand.

"Do you know where SD is?" Ruby had asked. She was intuitive for a bio, understanding the meaning behind some of his untranslatable tones.

Ruby had asked this simple question, and Disto chose not to answer it. He responded by saying he would tell her later. He wished he could have emitted the following:

"Unfortunately, yes. He's prepping for another off-world mission."

"You say that as if it's out of the ordinary. He *is* a driver," AT would have responded with.

Disto found that he could imagine how the conversation might have proceeded from there.

"He's a Driver that *should* be temporarily relieved of his responsibilities," Disto would say next. "We must get to him before he leaves."

Ruby, brave and always willing to help would offer, "Where do we have to go?"

"I'll retrieve SD from his ship," Disto said and then continued to lay out the next steps. "SD should be in the process of prepping for departure at this moment, if I understand pre-mission procedures. You'll meet us at the entrance to the Hall of Templates. Ruby, I suggest you retrieve Pippa."

Disto had trouble predicting what Ruby would say about that, but no matter what, Disto imagined he would have been honest with her and would have said things like, "I have concerns about Pippa. But its use will likely outweigh its non-use. Simple logical calculation."

Disto tried making a more advanced calculation that would predict the likelihood that Ruby would protest. His simulation was inconclusive. There were too many factors to account for regarding Bio behavior and even though he was confident he had a reasonable mapping of Ruby, minor things could yield wildly different results.

Additionally, he didn't know if Ruby noticed Pippa's strange behavior coming to the same conclusion as he—that Pippa was in contact with another robot and potentially providing information about their activities and plans.

No matter what, Disto's logical deduction stood on its own merit. Any usefulness Pippa might have outweighed any concerns.

He wished he had said all of that before they parted ways. Instead, he was on his way to get SD. He imagined Ruby finally asking him, "You're sure you're okay getting SD?"

Disto had gotten used to the way Ruby showed that she cared, so it wasn't a difficult prediction that she'd as this.

"Yes," Disto imagined saying, trying to envision sounding one hundred percent more confident than he felt.

Chapter 23

> Ruby <

"What do I say?" Ruby asked AT as she sat in front of the computer and camera. "And why would a bunch of robots who've never met me do what I say?"

Left arm at her side, she grabbed it with her right hand and tapped her foot. Her takeaway from the last time she was broadcast all over the news was that it gave her a queasy feeling in her chest. How can chests feel queasy, anyway?

How can chests feel queasy, how can robots feel afraid—or any emotion for that matter—and how could she, Ruby Palmer, feel like she could save the operating system of an entire planet of robots like some intergalactic tech support genius?

She briefly considered all of the brain tests she had been subjected to as part of growing up on Astroll 2, and how they determined that she wasn't mentally developed enough to be out on her own. Maybe they were right, and she had no business being here and was in way over her head.

Her chest was queasy, her brain was immature, and a robot historian was guiding her through this. It made perfect sense in the way playing ping-pong on the surface of the Sun doesn't.

"Tell them the facts as you know it. Be logical. Everyone responds to logic."

Ruby's mouth turned up at that. That might be true here,

but not where she was from. Back home, people typically attempted to turn logic around to suit their agenda or to sell something. She knew that a lot of people couldn't recognize the logic of a door, propping them open when they were meant to be shut, and often not even reading the sign with simple, one-word instructions on how to open it.

Unless it came with a celebrity endorsement.

The corner of her mouth inadvertently turned up. Here, on Location Zero, she *was* a celebrity.

"I know what to say. Let's get this started."

"Don't forget to tell them where to go."

"Of course."

"And when."

"Got it," Ruby said. "But wait… if *everyone* knows when and where, won't it be easier for them to try and stop us?"

"They may show up, but we will be performing actions so far beyond what their programming can handle, they won't be able to stop us."

Ruby nodded contemplatively, "I hope you're right."

"I am. And also make sure to tell them how this is for the benefit of our entire planet."

"Yep."

Ruby hit a button, and a light indicated that the camera was recording. She could edit out the bit where she took a few breaths before speaking.

> Sincere Proxy 891 <

Sincere Proxy was plugged in to a console accessing details of his next assignment when an unexpected tone signaled an alert message.

The message, in the form of a news broadcast, began with an image of Ruby Palmer—the Bio. He remembered Ruby Palmer as a companion to an unusual robot he was responsible for apprehending. Shortly after, she had performed some sort of illusory code, and ever since apprehending robots for storage violations accounted for only ten percent of his assignments instead of nearly eighty-two percent.

After the broadcast, he disconnected from the console, set his internal stopwatch to countdown to the time that he needed to be at the Hall of Templates.

> Fastidious Mechanic 719 <

Fastidious Mechanic's belly rumbled wildly, then settled into a calm vibration as he was machining a part needed to repair a kiosk that had suffered at the hands of a robot crash. He was perched on a floor in Inner Nonagon, engaged in helping to reconfigure the already destroyed space into a new set of kiosks. Although it was baffling since this region already had more kiosks than were in use, and he was certain that this space already had the maximum allocation per the standard.

His musings on the subject were interrupted when the screens that were set to continuously broadcast several news stations stopped to broadcast something new.

It was a message from Ruby.

The other robots on site all gave him a glance. It was known that Fastidious Mechanic was one of the robots who helped Ruby and as such he was easily recognized.

Fastidious Mechanic's belly stopped vibrating simultaneously with the end of Ruby's broadcast message. He opened it up, used his nimble appendage to pull out the newly created part, and set it down next to the robot who asked for it.

In this moment, he became aware that all the other robots on site were staring at him.

This made him uncomfortable. He didn't like to be the center of attention. But they were clearly all waiting for him to speak. To react.

He couldn't tell them what he was thinking.

What is the Bio doing? Does she know the havoc a message like this could cause?

He couldn't help but imagine a mess of restless robots, broken parts, and utter chaos.

The best he could bring himself to do was remain temperate, protect the Bio, and then go back to producing part after part in his belly.

"Of course, I'll be there at the right time. And I encourage all of you to do the same."

The robots all around him made tones and beeps of approval. If Fastidious Mechanic, one of Ruby's close companions on this world, supported her, so would they.

> Explosive Healer <

Moments ago, Explosive Healer finished conducting her third group session in 10000 tics and was starting to settle in to her contemplative alone time to attempt to create an art piece. Her inspiration was that of a simple series of circuits. The text would read, 'Energize Each Other.'

She was quite proud of the idea, but was interrupted by a message.

She was no longer in the right head space for art and all the robots in the Rejuvenation Region were supremely agitated.

She took up a centralized location in the Rejuvenation Region and chirped loudly, "All robots who want to join in on this new and turbulent struggle… follow me!"

> Austere Agent <

Austere Agent replayed the message to the other agents.

There was Ruby, the Bio, on the screen and they all watched in a combination of awe and horror:

"Robots," the human began, "you know me as someone who has helped you in the recent past. I want to help you again. Help me help you. Help me help all of you.

"There is data corruption happening in your major Halls. Many of you have probably noticed the effects, without realizing exactly what you were seeing. My robot friends and I understand the problem, and we have an algorithm that we can use to patch the Hall that will fix it.

"There are a handful of robots that don't want us to fix

anything because they don't see that there are any problems, or they're afraid that they're losing control. But we have to put fears and doubt aside and do what's right... and logical, of course. We need to show up to the Hall—all of us—and force them to let us apply the patch. This will only work if every able-bodied robot joins us.

"When I came to this planet, I was a stranger to all of you. And I for one, had terrible opinions about robots. But I was able to open my mind, my central processing unit, to other ideas and overcome my original programming so much so that I've come to call this place...well, it almost feels like home. This place feels like a part of me. I don't know if that will make much sense to any of you, but...well, just know that I like being here and want to see this place, and see you all thrive. I was told to appeal to logic in this message, but I've come to know that robots are more than just logic. Location Zero is filled with robots that are smart, kind, funny, and a lot of other things that I never imagined robots could be. You protected me, and now I want to protect *you*

"We'll be at the entrance to the Hall of Templates, waiting for you to join us, at 444 tics from the end of this message."

The screen went blank.

Prodigal Agent said, "let's watch it again."

"That was already the fourth time. It's time to decide what to do."

"Exactly what it says. Meet her at the Hall of Templates. If she has a fix..."

"We can't trust her. She's a bio," Austere Agent said.

"But she's helped us before," said Flashy Agent.

"And look where that got us? Look at the problems that created?" Austere Agent countered.

"I don't know—it seems that the only downside is that more robots know that there are problems," said Smooth Agent.

"Exactly! Robots can't know. If they know, they'll worry, they'll malfunction with confusion, and they won't execute their assignments. Everything will quickly deteriorate turn into complete chaotics," Austere Agent pleaded.

"That's a little overly dramatic, don't you think?"

"Dramatic? Smooth Agent, you're not grasping this. The Agent lines exist to help keep chaos at bay. If we can't execute that assignment, we will be out of reasons to exist. We'll be discontinued." Austere Agent couldn't believe he was having to argue with his colleagues.

"That's quite dramatic as well…" Flashy Agent looked to Smooth Agent who smoothly raised and lowered his chassis slightly, "but we see your point."

"So, we'll be at the Hall. But to stop her."

"But what about fixing the data corruption?" Prodigal Agent, who had been quiet this whole time, finally added.

"That's someone else's problem—a robot's problem in another agency."

"But if she already has an algorithm…?"

"If a simple human can figure it out, so can the robots of the Agency of Algorithms. It is not her job to perform, it is as simple as that." Austere Agent was quite sure of that fact.

All the other agents except for Prodigal Agent nodded in agreement.

"It's agreed. We'll show up early. Be there to guard the place before they get there."

"What if they think we might show up early and they show up even earlier?" Smooth Agent asked.

Austere Agent took a fraction of a tic to think that over. "Well, we'll go even earlier than that."

"What if they think that's what we'll calculate, and they'll show up even earlier?"

"Let's stop this circular logic. Let's go right now and wait."

Again, nods all around. Except for Prodigal Agent, who sat in quiet contemplation.

"Follow me…" said Austere Agent and led the group out the door.

Chapter 24

> Detailed Historian <

There were no indicators that SD's ship was about to launch as Disto boarded the lift to take him there. That was a good sign—a sign that he had arrived early enough.

As he stepped off the lift and into the rear of the space reserved for the driver's slot, he saw exactly what he had hoped to see: Swell Driver.

SD was perched in front of the consoles. His coloring was static and pale at two threets. Very unusual to be so static. The shimmer that glowed from most robots had turned dull, and it made Disto uncomfortable. Something was still very wrong with SD.

Disto indicated his presence with a soft tone. He didn't like sneaking up on his friend, or anyone for that matter.

SD made a tone in response. A minor acknowledgment of Disto's proximity.

"What are you doing?" Disto asked as he approached carefully.

"I don't know," SD replied. "I thought I was taking Ruby home. They told me to come here."

"Who is *they*?" Disto asked.

Disto wasn't sure SD heard him since SD didn't answer. Disto approached a little more and heard SD softly say, "I have the star map..."

Disto abruptly stopped. "You do? Can I see it?"

SD touched a button on his console, and a large screen began to illuminate in front of them. Disto didn't simply stare at it; he recorded what he was seeing and compared it to the last star map he had looked at with Ruby. Yes, this one was different. Could he be sure it was the original?

"Where did you get this?"

"It's been in my local storage ever since I found Ruby. This was not standard procedure. But the place seemed special and something inside of me…wanted to hold on to it."

They both stared at it in silence. Disto briefly wished he was better versed in the subtle differences between solar systems, including his own. Maybe there was a module extension he could download. For historical purposes, of course.

Ruby walked in, looking with a particular sense of wonder and curiosity that Disto couldn't miss. SD continued to look down, not flinching at her presence.

"Is that crazy? Am I crazy?" SD asked.

"No, you're a lifesaver!" Ruby said.

SD looked up, startled by her presence. For a moment, he appeared relieved at her proximity, but this quickly reverted to a state of worry.

"Where's AT?" Disto asked.

"He's waiting at the entrance to the lift. Can I get in here and see this?" Ruby stepped in closer and put her hand on SD's chassis while she looked up at the screen. Disto observed that Ruby's touch had no effect on SD. He was still the same static and pale two threets.

Disto looked up at the screen once more. This was the longest he had ever stared at one. Star maps were used to navigate interstellar space. They had nothing to do with his function as a historian. Yes, he and other robots were aware that stars moved and galaxies shifted over time, but at a scale that was not relevant. Even if he was active for billions of tics, the movement of the stars would still be irrelevant.

As such, he was not all that knowledgeable about the cosmos at all. Or his own star system. He saw it on the map, highlighted at four threets and with the symbol that represented Location Zero. In one corner was a legend, and from the data represented there, he could tell that they were looking at a region of space that was almost 500 light-years wide, high, and deep.

"Can you enlarge our present location?" Disto asked SD.

SD did as asked, and the screen was now largely occupied by a star and several orbits. One of the orbits had a dot and the Location Zero symbol over it.

There were three other orbits with their own symbols over them.

"What are those?" Disto asked.

"Those are the other planets that orbit our host star," SD answered with no inflection in his tone.

"Have you been to them?"

"Oh yes. Each of them several times. There are robots stationed at each performing mining operations. There are routine swaps of materials. I have performed that mission many times."

Disto correlated this with information he had on his world's history. It didn't correlate. "How long have they been operating?" he asked.

"Longer than I've been operating."

That explained it. It must be part of the missing information. But he was surprised that he hadn't heard about anything involving these stations recently.

Disto continued to look at the map, thinking of the possibilities to expand his line of historical research when and if they could find the historical records. When were these facilities established? By whom? And why? These questions gnawed at him. He was a historian, after all. But as usual, they would have to wait until the current crisis, not a historical one, concluded.

As Disto continued his examination of the map, his focus settled on an area composed of several line segments. Each segment was dim compared to the rest of the map features but connected to form the outline of a curved rectangle. The location of this rectangle was the same orbit as Location Zero from its host star but on the opposite side of that star from Location Zero.

As Location Zero moved, so did this shape.

"What is that?" Disto asked, using his appendage to point at the shifting shape.

"The Keep Out Zone. The other pilots and I call it the KOZ."

"What is it?" Disto asked.

"Exactly what it says. A keep-out zone. We keep out."

"Why?" This was the next of many questions forming in Disto's circuits.

"I don't know. I was never programmed with that information."

"And you never asked?" Ruby chimed in. Disto was so engrossed in understanding the map's details that he almost forgot she was there.

"Why would I ask?"

SD made a good point. It was out of the nature of SD's programming to ask questions like that.

"*Can* you ask?" Ruby said. Disto enjoyed witnessing this pilot-to-pilot interaction and hoped it would be more productive than his non-pilot input. Ruby was also programmed as a pilot, so maybe she would have some greater insight.

"No."

"And there's no explanation you could possibly think of?" Ruby's brow was now furrowed.

SD just stared at her.

"No."

Ruby made a motion with her arms and shoulders that Disto interpreted as an indication that her question queue was empty.

Disto had to remember the robot they were dealing with. Disto was programmed to ask questions—most robots, especially any Driver, were not—particularly the 'why' question. This bothered his circuits because he was filled with questions that began with 'why.' Why was there a keep-out zone? Why would someone add such a feature? Why was the location perfectly positioned from where they were? *His* question queue was full.

He would archive this queue—this puzzle—for later... Disto returned his attention back to the present.

"SD, you have to come with us. We have to go to the Hall of Templates."

"But I have to take Ruby home."

"Yes, you will. After we've dealt with the Hall of Templates."

> Ruby <

Ruby secured her ponytail and narrowed her eyes at the entrance to the Hall of Templates. AT at her side, they moved with purpose. Disto and SD had left SD's ship a few minutes ahead of her. She wanted to take a moment or two to inspect the work done on *Apple Pi* to reassemble it, but Disto informed her that little had been put back together. But once this was all over, it didn't matter. She would still get home, whether or not *Apple Pi* was operable.

They needed to get through this final challenge. Here, at the entrance to the Hall of Templates she'd heard so much about, she was mildly disappointed. She imagined the entrance would be a little grander, the way the robots talked in reverence about the place. Like she expected it to be the entrance to a Gothic cathedral seen in several old movies, maybe even like the ancient Notre Dame that only existed in pictures and vids.

In retrospect, that didn't make sense. They were on Level 3, and the ceiling height was consistent throughout the level... which wasn't terribly high at all, not when compared to Notre Dame. Maybe 15 feet by Ruby's judgment.

The place was packed with robots, so it was difficult to even approach the place.

AT helped pave their way through so they could get to the front. He made a series of beeps and tones that indicated they were there, and as soon as robots saw who it was—Ruby, the Bio—they parted to let them pass through.

Ruby took in the diversity of robots that were present. Most of which she had caught glimpses of on newsfeeds, but now they were all here in front of her. She saw robots with varying numbers of chassis components, various appendages, and with a variety of outer artwork.

She even glimpsed a few robots that looked more like AT, soft and malleable. They looked as if the crowd could crush them. But AT didn't seem worried.

They approached the front of the crowd. Again, the entrance to the Hall was quite underwhelming. A series of three kiosks guarded the entrance to a door. A robot manned each kiosk. They looked identical to each other and not too dissimilar from the kiosks in that they were slim and tall. If it wasn't for their appendages that resembled arms and that they weren't bolted to the ground like the kiosks, they could easily have been mistaken for kiosks themselves.

"I counted 1024 robots," AT whispered to her.

"That doesn't include Disto or SD. I don't see them," Ruby said. She did see Quiet Painter, Fastidious Mechanic, and several other robots she knew. Austere Agent was even there, way up front.

They were all staring at her. Waiting. Ruby turned her back to them, mostly so she didn't have to stare back, and instead focused on the kiosks and the robots.

"Hello," she said. She wasn't sure if she was talking to the kiosk or the robot.

"Greetings!" the central kiosk responded. "Welcome to the Hall of Templates, Prime Office."

Ruby looked at AT. AT shrugged. Ruby wasn't sure if it was comforting to know that one of the smartest robots she had met also wasn't certain what to do next.

"We've come to apply a patch," she said.

"I cannot comply with that request. Please see the main menu for options. Say 'audio' if you would like me to repeat them."

The screen on the top of all three kiosks displayed a main menu. Perhaps there was an option that would lead to another option that would lead to another that would eventually allow them to do what they needed to do without any difficulties. She wasn't even remotely optimistic about this, but perhaps this would be easier than they had planned for. Perhaps, the swarm of robots wasn't necessary at all. Perhaps this would be quick and painless.

She read through the menu.

It had three options:

'1. Initiate request 2. Reapply template 3. Return to start.'

It didn't escape her notice that the menu was presented in both her language and with the equivalent robotic symbols next to them. They auto-detected who she was, apparently.

Ruby began with the most benign of the options. 'Return to start.' It took her to a welcome screen and in the bottom corner was the symbol for 'menu.' Pressing it took her, unsurprisingly, back to the menu.

Next, she tried 'initiate request.' The kiosk blared a sound that clearly indicated she did something wrong, and it spoke: "Error. We are unable to process a request for a new robot. Unable to determine robot family."

Disto appeared at her side. SD was with him.

"You are not a robot. You can only initiate the request to have a robot within a line of robots related to you. For example, I could have another Detailed Historian created, or even a Circumstantial Historian. See?"

Disto returned to the main menu, and when he touched, 'Initiate,' a list of robots came up. 'Circumstantial Historian' was indeed in the list, as was Misunderstood Recorder, Filthy Biographer and a host of others. Excellent Collector was listed, too.

"How does this help us?" Ruby asked.

"It doesn't," Disto responded. He turned and addressed the robot standing behind the kiosk in their native tonal language.

The robot, previously useless and inert, came to life. He turned the kiosk to face him, which shocked Ruby. She had assumed it was statically bolted to the ground.

His appendages poked at the screen.

When he was done, he returned the kiosk to its initial position and produced some additional noises.

Disto's color indicated that he was not pleased but also not surprised.

"I attempted to make an appointment to see Hopeful Executive 421, head of the Hall."

"And you weren't successful," Ruby said.

"Would you have expected anything else?"

"I might have neglected to mention that I've been trying to get an appointment to meet with him for several days. However, this robot was kind enough to tell me that the Hopeful Executive is inside."

"So, we walk in?"

"No. They," Disto gestured at the robots standing at the kiosks in a hushed tone, "will not let us in. They are blocking us."

Ruby looked at the robots and back at Disto. They couldn't have exceeded six inches at their widest. They blocked nothing.

Why didn't they talk about this ahead of time? Ruby was not prepared to disable any robots.

"Can't we simply walk around them?"

Disto looked at her as if to say, "let me demonstrate," and attempted exactly that, moving in between the kiosks. As soon as he did, the three robots behind interlocked their appendages and their bodies had produced many more appendages to do so, creating a web.

Disto looked at Ruby as if to say, "See?"

"So, this is where we storm-" Ruby began.

Disto interrupted and brought her away from the kiosk robots. He instructed, "Not so loud, Ruby. They look inert, but I promise you they can hear you. But yes. We must disable the robots and storm in."

Again, why didn't they talk about this ahead of time? Sometimes Ruby forgot that each robot was so specified, they often faltered in skillsets outside their own. Disto was a

Historian, not a Planner or an Organizer—if there was even such a thing.

She was unprepared to disable any robots.

"What happens once we get inside?"

"You have the algorithm?"

"Yes. Crazy Porter converted it for us, and we've already distributed it to several robots. I have it in this storage thing you guys gave me," Ruby said as she held up the storage device that fit in the palm of her hand. "AT has a copy as well."

"Good," said Disto.

He made additional sounds. AT repeated them, and they stepped aside, pulling Ruby with them as a dozen of the largest robots approached and pulled the kiosk guard robots apart.

The robots were unable to protest or complain as their appendages were ripped up and sparked. The sounds of bending metal and the smell of melting plastic irritated all of Ruby's senses, particularly her nose, which clearly had complete control over her stomach and directed it to churn. It wasn't like seeing *Apple Pi* in its state of disassembly or a communicuff open and laid out on a table. This was utter and unmitigated carnage.

Ruby covered her mouth to muffle her gasp and leaned over to AT. "Will they be okay?"

AT whispered to her, "Perhaps. I will try my best to fix as many of them as I can at a later time."

Ruby looked at the mangled robot parts, splayed in the wrong directions, and wondered what exactly she had gotten herself into.

The robots started passing through the damaged guards and into the room beyond. Disto merged into the crowd, along with SD, and as AT began to move, he reached out for Ruby and pulled her along.

The room they entered was not what Ruby was expecting. She had imagined a crowded room full of robots active in whatever they did to keep the Hall of Templates running. Instead, it was practically empty from the entrance to the far side of the room where there were five kiosks and five robots, each behind its kiosk. What was all the empty space for? Then, the answer popped into her head as she remembered her experience on Astroll 2 getting her communicuff fixed.

Endless lines.

Ruby groaned internally.

Ruby made her way up to them along with AT, Disto, and SD.

"Have any of you ever been here before? Do you know what this is?"

"I have not, and I do not," Disto said. "Though I do fear those kiosks are extraordinarily unusual. Stay behind me, Ruby."

Chapter 25

> Ambitious Technician <

This was the most uncomfortable AT had ever been. There were many robots in a room that was not designed for many robots. He expected to leave the large mass of robots behind, but they also filled up this next room.

AT was holding onto a slew of questions. *How was the Hall of Templates a simple room like this? The kiosks must connect to the Core, but that's it?* This didn't make sense to AT, who was used to things making sense.

He looked at Disto, who expressed the same level of perplexedness. Robots were still entering the room, smushing all of them together. He had to let out some of the air from several of the individual components that made up his chassis, else he was going to pop, and he wasn't confident in the repair options in this region. If he was back in his home region, he might have been less cautious.

AT looked at Ruby next. He was also worried that she was going to pop. The Bios were also made of material that could not withstand all this external pressure.

"Disto! You need to tell them to stop!" He had to increase his volume to be heard over the ambient noise.

AT observed one robot successfully making its way to the front of the room. As this robot did, other robots around him gave him space. They parted to let him through.

"Austere Agent," Disto said, clearly intending to introduce him to the robots who did not recognize him.

"Yes," Austere Agent responded. "It seems that wherever I find you, I find Ruby as well." He nodded in Ruby's direction. "And why am I not surprised to find Swell Driver with you and *this one*..." Next, he nodded in AT's direction.

"This is good," Austere Agent continued. "I am here to inform you all that the request to return Ruby Palmer, the Bio, home in a method that allows Swell Driver's ship to interface with your 'space' 'station' has been granted. We would like you to leave immediately."

"When we're done here," Ruby said sternly. AT's circuits produced a not unpleasant warmth at hearing her speak up.

The warmth went away when Austere Agent looked directly at him.

"And let's talk about *this one*. Amateur Technician, yes? I know this one traveled far to get here. And I know what he brought with him." Austere Agent's tone indicated a belief that his voice was the only one that should be heard at the moment. That he was the most important robot in the room. AT didn't usually let robots like that irk him.

But AT wasn't sure what to say. Inside his soft circuits he was uneasy at being known and seen like this.

"You have a key," Austere Agent said. "I know which encryption algorithm it associates with. I also know that it's useless. Which is why you should disband now, return to your enclaves, all of you." He said this in Ruby's language. He then repeated it in a series of tones and chirps that every robot in sensing distance could hear.

"I was right. *Nowhere* is safe to speak freely. We are always being watched." Disto said with a tone unlike any AT had ever heard before. He registered it as outrage.

Austere Agent produced a short set of clicking tones and then a shattering, rapid amount of loud, high clicking tones. AT had never heard a robot make a noise quite like this. It made his insides feel as inflated as his outsides.

"Our communication systems are innovative. But you

shouldn't worry, Dysfunctional Historian. We will take care of any patches that need to be made. The Bio is now obsolete and will be sent home."

This time it was Disto who challenged him.

"You're overreaching," Disto said. "You are an Agent of the Agency of interfaces. As such, your responsibilities do not extend to encryption algorithms. That is for agents of another agency."

"Ah, but without successful encryption and decryption, an interface can be rendered useless. What you fail to understand, Disastrous Historian, is that the Agency of Interfaces is involved in everything, everywhere. We might be the most important Agency in all the Core. As such, we have reach into every agency and Hall." He produced more tones, but this time they were low pitched and more drawn out. "We know everything. In fact, I find it highly entertaining that so many other robots have lost so much knowledge of our culture and history. Even Historians, like you. Take un-connected communications, for example. I find it highly entertaining that the knowledge of our capabilities in that area has been lost among the masses."

AT looked at Disto and Ruby, who were looking at each other and back. He sensed Austere Agent was not providing all the information he had.

"Do you mean wireless communications? I've been here for several weeks with wireless—pur-fi—equipment and haven't detected anything. What frequency is this mysterious comms at?" Ruby asked, with her appendages crossed in front of her.

By now, some breathing room had opened up, and a circle had formed around Ruby, AT, and Disto. They weren't going to be smushed after all.

"It's on an electromagnetic frequency of seven-point-eight gigahertz—I think is the correct translation that your kind of Bio would understand," Austere Agent said, staring at Ruby but waving his hand around the room, "which is not something that any robot is equipped to pick up. Only our console equipment. All you robots think all communication is wired, but it is not."

"That's a common frequency where I come from. So common, in fact, that it is the backbone of our primary network... but..." she trailed off, and AT watched the flesh around her optical sensors open up, and he could see more of those sensors than he had before. If she had a light on her chassis, it would be incredibly active.

But she did sort of have a light on her chassis. It was part of the device on her arm that housed Pippa.

"Ruby, I think Pippa is trying to..." started AT, but Ruby was already looking at her.

AT and the others all looked at the flashing indicator light on Ruby's communicuff. She held it up for the group to witness whatever she was going to do with it.

"Pippa?" she spoke to it.

There was a pause, and then, "Ruby! You noticed my light!"

"Yes, Pippa. Have you been in contact with someone over the pur-fi frequency?"

"Yes. His name is Invisible Scout."

"Why didn't you tell me this before?"

"You never asked. And my trust factor settings—"

Ruby connected the hand that did not have the communicuff attached to it with the smooth portion of her head above her visual sensors.

"I shouldn't have to ask for you to tell me important things like that. Never mind right now. We'll talk about this later."

"What kind of AI is this?" AT whispered to Disto.

"Not a terribly intelligent one," Disto said. "Humans can only create very limited AI. They should stick to their typical forms of reproduction to create other intelligent Bios. Although, from my discussions with Ruby, apparently that is nearly as imprecise with no guarantee as to the resulting intelligence levels."

"Speaking of imprecise... where is SD?"

AT and Disto looked around and didn't see him on their initial scan. He must be locked in the crowd.

The crowd was fidgety. The hum of servo motors, big and

small, waiting to move was at an uncomfortable decibel level. AT could tell that Disto detected it as well.

AT wanted to be more proactive instead of waiting. Austere Agent still stood there, silent, with his appendages crossed in front of his chassis in a way that indicated he concluded he had already won.

Won what? AT thought. *How can he, representative of the Agency of Interfaces, think that leaving malfunctioning algorithms and corrupted data in place was acceptable?*

Once again, as if she was able to read the data in his circuits, Ruby stated loudly to all the robots that could hear her, "Does anyone here think that leaving malfunctioning algorithms and corrupted data in place is a good idea?" The robots that understood her shouted, "No!" and translated for the other robots, so there was a second wave of, "No!" a moment later.

Austere Agent was surveying the crowd, not looking over at him or Disto. AT flashed a red light on the backside of a robot that was standing in front of Disto. Disto flashed back an indicator in response.

"I'm going to access the kiosk," AT said in flashy red that only Disto—or anyone so equipped—would be able to understand.

Everyone's attention was on Ruby, on Austere Agent, and not on themselves or the third kiosk, the one over to the side.

"Agreed, but what will you do," Disto asked.

"What I do best," said AT. "Fix broken things. In this case, by replacing one key with another."

"I don't think I followed how that will work."

"Remember there are two separate but related problems going on here. One is that data is, in fact, getting corrupted. Ruby has the algorithm to fix that.

"But the second problem is that the key that is used to unencrypt some data is *also* corrupted. So, some data seems like it's corrupted, but it's not. It can't be unencrypted without the right key. I have that."

Disto flashed a series of red dots to indicate he understood, and that AT should certainly not waste another tic explaining

173

anything more to him.

AT was already plugged in discreetly to the kiosk. His soft chassis allowed him greater flexibility, and he could deflate a long thin appendage that was usually hidden but reserved for those hard-to-reach spaces. It wrapped around the kiosk and plugged in out of view of nearly everyone in the room.

Nearly. Since that's when Austere Agent looked over with recognition at what AT was doing—although AT suspected that he received a warning, wirelessly, since apparently, that was a thing that existed.

"Disto, look!" Disto was luckily still able to see his red dots.

Disto did, in fact, look and rushed in-between AT and the path of a hefty Agent who was accelerating towards them.

Nearby robots quickly coordinated to join Disto. One by one and then all at once, the robots surrounded Disto with their metal or inflatable bodies. Tall or squat lengths, they huddled around Disto without anyone saying a word.

AT tried to force his way into a processor with an alternate, technical accessing route. The kiosks were notoriously ornery about that, and naturally, they obliviously complained.

"Halt your action," they repeated. "This is an incorrect procedure…"

Disto, Quiet Painter, and others formed two semicircles— one around AT, protecting him, and one surrounding Austere Agent to keep him from going anywhere.

The kiosk's processor finally let him make the kind of connection that was common for someone engaged in repair work. From there, AT could access several unfamiliar functions buried in layers upon layers of outdated patches. As he poked around, he felt bad for the poor kiosk. It had not undergone any maintenance in at least a few million tics, maybe more.

No wonder it resisted his access attempt. It wasn't used to the connection.

Behind him, robots clamored against Austere Agent, the sound of metal scraping against metal and aggressive beeping filled the room.

As AT searched through the layers, small sparks tickled his circuitry and in his chassis. Time was dwindling.

He also knew that he was the wrong Technician for this job. If it had been a matter of crisscrossed wires, he was the right robot to repair that. But this was code, and there were never Programmer robots around... well... ever. But Ruby...

As if she sensed she was needed, she was by his side and had folded in her lower appendages to bring her sensor and vocal actuator close to where AT had made the connection to the kiosk.

"AT, talk to me," she said.

AT didn't respond. He continued to open the layers and functions one by one.

Everything he encountered had a layer that was sponsored by the Hall of Performance and Metrics. He had no idea that Hall had deployed functions everywhere... but now wasn't the time to ruminate on such things.

Agency of Restoration—interesting, since that was AT's agency, but not what he was looking for.

Agency of Testing, Unit Test Review... not sure, they could hold off Austere Agent for a while, but there were other agents, and they might arrive soon as well.

Agency of Algorithms... Reduction subdivision. Closer, but still not it.

AT imagined turning around and seeing the metal shells and exposed wires that once belonged to his new friends. It was up to him to find what he needed and minimize the damage. And repair the rest later.

Why was there a metric on how many robots approved of this metric?

AOA Encryption Map null-null-one.

Got it.

A connection to Agency of Algorithms, Encryption subdivision. Despite its name, everything about it was exposed. The keys were not, though. They were kept several levels deep in the memory structure and the master key was guarded by a little algorithm—a puzzle of logic.

The algorithm provided the details of its puzzle to AT through a series of low tones nearly out of his hearing range, "This task is outside of your programming, and the typical penalty for accessing it is reprogramming. You must respond with a true or false statement. If your statement is true, you will be reprogrammed. If your statement is false, you will be sent to Resource Allocation Agency for disassembly. If your statement can neither be proven to be true nor false, you may continue on with your task."

AT dared not produce an utterance. He knew that security puzzles such as this would take any statement he made next to be *the* statement he was supposed to respond with. He had to think this through carefully.

He could think of many statements that were obviously true, such as "I am AT," and many statements that were equally obvious as untruths, like "I am a Bio." One that was neither was...

"I will be sent to the Resource Allocation Agency for disassembly," AT responded, making sure to use the exact wording from the puzzle. His ah-ha moment was in realizing that he could prove the present, and maybe even the past, but the future was wide open with uncertainty—it could not be true or false until it happened.

The algorithm didn't respond immediately. This worried AT, who was quite proud of his answer. Then, the algorithm shut down, allowing AT to continue.

He replaced the master key with his.

All of this took less than 50 tics.

AT disconnected from the kiosk, and returning his attention to the robots, saw a partially dismantled Austere Agent and an inert Quiet Painter.

Chapter 26

> Ruby <

All Ruby could do was wait... and watch what was happening. She was not about to get in the middle of several robots who were clearly capable of damaging her beyond repair. So, she couldn't help.

Pippa was the one who was downloading the EPADAC algorithm to the Core. There wasn't anything Ruby could do to help there, either.

Still, Ruby wasn't sure they should be trusting this 'Invisible Scout.' This robot's name even sounded like it shouldn't be trusted.

'Invisible.' Invisible how? From what? Could it be an alias of sorts?

"Ruby," Pippa said, "Scout has provided me with the instructions for communicating with the Core's gate agent."

"Why didn't I have to communicate with a gate agent when I implemented the original compression algorithm?" Ruby asked.

There was a pause. Pippa was relaying the question to Scout and getting a response. It was the briefest of pauses, only long enough to have this pithy thought.

"Because you went around the standard interface," Pippa said. "Since then, they've updated the interface to be wider stretched throughout various systems and locations. They've essentially updated their security because of you."

Ruby replied. "But I did something that *helped* them."

Pippa responded, "Yes, you did. But think about it from their perspective. If they're that susceptible to someone coming in and making changes to their system, that's a security threat. Lucky for them, you were trying to help, but what if you weren't?"

"Oh." Ruby said. This made too much sense. She had never meant to elicit any kind of *fear*. She tucked a stray hair behind her ears and stared at the floor for a moment.

"What do I have to do?" Ruby asked.

"In the interest of time, I should probably do it, and update you afterwards."

Again, that made too much sense to Ruby. And once again, all she could do was wait.

Waiting—especially patiently—was not one of Ruby's strengths.

She looked around once more for anyone else she could help.

AT disconnected from the kiosk and was looking... flushed—for a robot. Disto was trying to get the crowd to disperse. Austere Agent had been dismantled, at least to the point where he couldn't do anything. She could see that the face screen on his chassis was still active, which meant that he could likely be repaired. Quiet Painter's chassis lay inert on the ground next to him. Ruby's stomach knotted up as she assumed he wasn't in as good condition.

Where was SD?

Ruby looked around and didn't see him. He probably got stuck in the previous room. Ruby hoped he was okay...

She hoped her family was okay, too. She should have been home by now, passing on what she'd learned about the software upgrades that could get them killed. She hoped beyond hope that they hadn't set out for Earth yet. Not before she could get back there.

But the ache in her heart was telling her that it was probably too late.

178

Her heart pressed inwards into her chest, and Ruby shook her head of the thought that she couldn't bear. This wasn't an option. She had to focus on what she could do, and she *couldn't* just stand and wait—there had to be something she could do.

"Pippa," she said.

"I'm busy," Pippa responded.

"I know. And I need to help. At least light up this one remaining console so I can see what's going on."

She took a position in front of one of the kiosks that had managed to remain undamaged and poked at the menu.

"Here, Pippa. I want to see what's going on here." She had been in the Core before and was familiar with the structure. If she could access the main menu from here, she could navigate and find her way around.

"But Ruby," Pippa began.

"No buts. Get it up on the display."

"Ruby, I'm already done deploying the algorithm."

That was quick! Ruby thought. "Oh. Well, then... next order of business. Let's go make sure SD is okay."

> Swell Driver <

SD wasn't able to push himself to the front to stay near Ruby and Disto. Not that he tried too hard. This was not his area of expertise, and he knew it. He knew his responsibility was to protect the star map in his memory until he could escort Ruby home.

By now, more agents had come, and they were being taken care of by the crowd. One by one, the mob of robots stopped the agents in their path and either warded them off with sheer fear or took them on. They fought with numbers, with force, and without hesitation.

So, he let the crowd move him around within the room. He hoped he would be alright if he didn't fight against it. There was certainly no path out, so he searched for an opening to be pushed off to the side of the room, where he could stagnate.

SD found an opening and went for it. He swiveled around

a robot and dashed towards an empty space, lining the wall. Only, he was a little too late, and the crowd began to swallow him again. He could feel the mass pushing him undesirably, until…

A tug.

Something had grabbed onto him, tugging him into an open space.

SD looked up, and his visual sensors met with Explosive Healer's.

"SD, I've got you!" Explosive Healer beeped, and SD's internal sensors registered that he was not in danger of tipping over, so he could lean into Explosive Healer's pull from her single appendage. Together, they managed to root SD out of the chaos. Explosive Healer rushed SD behind a fallen kiosk, where they'd be safe.

"Are you alright?" she said. She wasn't looking directly at him but the crowd. She stared at the crowd with a studied, focused screen. SD recognized that look on Explosive Healer and wondered if she knew she was not staring at a painting. "This is a unique experience, is it not?" she asked before SD could answer her first question.

And before he could answer this one, she continued, as if jumping from thought to thought. This conversation was rooted in something that SD couldn't recognize nor completely understand. It was beyond him.

"I brought all the robots from the Rejuvenation Region who were sufficiently mobile and alert with me," she said and gestured to a few of the robots that were nearby.

"Is that safe?" SD asked. "For them, I mean."

"Swell Driver, I commend you for your concern in the safety of others. That is the sort of thought that is needed to keep us not only functioning but thriving."

A robot bumped into SD from the side. SD's chassis lit up with surprise for a moment, but the robot left them both unscathed. Robots were still making their way into the room that had opened up beyond the kiosks. How many robots could possibly fit in that space beyond? Probably less than were trying to get in.

SD wondered aloud, "Considering each robot's self-preservation functions. It isn't logical for this many robots to be here. It isn't safe."

"Yes, of course," said Explosive Healer, who was watching other robots slam into each other at unsafe speeds and with amounts of force that could damage extended appendages or worse...

"Why did you come to us, Swell Driver? What, truly, was your goal in coming to the Rejuvenation Region?"

That was simple. Ruby brought him. That's why he went. But why did she bring him? He tried to remember and failed.

He was only able to recall a worried look on Ruby's face.

Previous to that, he remembered tiny snippets. A console of a ship that wasn't his. A klaxon going off in a ship, maybe the same ship? It also wasn't his. A planet that felt... nearby. Code in his system that didn't belong to him but that he needed for some reason.

Remembering these images sped up his processors like the discomfort he registered when someone else was driving his ship. *When had that happened?* It had indeed happened, it made him immensely uncomfortable to try and access those memories, and he couldn't remember the details. He didn't like thinking about any of it.

Explosive Healer touched her appendage to SD's chassis, and the uncomfortable images ceased to form. His processors started to slow down.

This was why he had come to the Rejuvenation Region.

All those images, the memories, they bothered his circuits. To the point that he sped up yet froze. And there was something that he couldn't identify preventing him from telling anyone about them. It was all confusing, and paralyzing, and completely isolating. He wanted to reset without the side effects of a full factory reset. He worried that he might get swallowed up in the disconcerting memories like he almost got swallowed up in the crowd of hostile robots.

Both times, Explosive Healer was there.

Getting his mind off of it, forgetting all about it, was what he was learning in the Rejuvenation Region before remembering the star map.

He still had the map, and he still had to help her.

SD could sense that Explosive Healer was no longer paying attention to the chaos of robotic movement around them. She was still touching his chassis, and her attention was solely focused on him.

She asked, "How does one final session sound?"

"Right now?" SD's screen twitched as the sight of a large, orange spark flashed in the center of the room.

Explosive Healer said, "It'll be short. One single question."

SD tilted downwards, signaling for her to proceed. He leaned forward and held still, waiting for her to speak.

"Why, SD?" she asked. Before SD could ask what she even meant by that, Explosive Healer provided the context. "Throughout all the work we've done together, I still see you wallowing about. Your disappointment in yourself is clearer than a polished window. Why?"

SD's processors began to speed up. "I...I don't know."

"Yes, you do. It's the hardest thing for a robot to face. Not fulfilling their duties. But I looked into your background. You are the most marvelous of all the Swell Drivers, performing your duties and functions splendidly. So, what is it that you blame yourself for?"

The numbness in his chassis began to dissolve, and it was slowly replaced with a rippling pain. Like a thousand notifications were going off at once inside of him, and he couldn't check any of them because if he did, he would know what he wasn't supposed to know.

SD shifted back and forth, "That's not what it is."

Explosive Healer moved closer to SD and asked, "Why do you blame yourself?"

The kiosk they hid behind was hit by an Agent ramming into it. SD and Explosive Healer moved back barely enough to get out of the way.

"How could I not?" SD cried, "There's something wrong

inside of me, and I don't know why it's there! And if I could have remembered…" All of the energy inside of SD couldn't stay put any longer. The exterior of his chassis increased in temperature, and for the first time in a while, his face-screen wasn't a solid color, but a mix of threets morphing together—shades of all the planets he'd flown by and nebulas he'd flown through. He said, "If I could have remembered, then maybe Ruby would have been able to go home! Maybe none of this would have happened!

Healer touched SD's chassis once again. "Ask yourself: will it change the outcome? Will blaming yourself change anything?"

Explosive Healer's face screen flashed yellow, and she pushed SD to the wall. SD began to tip over but regained balance and looked towards Healer. An agent was fleeing from a group of charging robots, and SD and Healer had been right in the path, but now only Healer remained.

"Healer!" SD shouted, but it was too late. He lunged forward, but the outskirts of the crowd got the better of him, and SD was pushed back towards the wall. Once the agent was motionless, the crowd dispersed.

SD only needed to roll a little bit before he saw her.

Explosive Healer lay smushed under several robots that were still moving, trying to get to the front of the room. The agent was a few feet away, nearly detached, still, and face-screen completely dark.

Explosive Healer was completely inert.

Chapter 27

> Ruby <

"Nothing seems any different," Ruby said to her friends. They were all in the Inner Nonagon. Ruby sat crossed-legged on the floor with her back to a wall. They were in a spot that allowed them to 'robot-watch,' as Ruby called it, after explaining how she used to 'people-watch' on the ring-walk back on Astroll 2.

"But things *are* different," Disto said. "We're more confident, for one. Knowing that our data is correct. The Hall of Performance and Metrics is reporting that algorithm execution confidence has never been higher!"

Ruby looked around. She didn't see it. She observed robots moving from one end of the Inner Nonagon to the other. Some robots were plugged into kiosks, and others were chatting with each other.

On the far end, the splashes of color on several panels were getting replaced with other splashes of color. While she didn't know what it meant, she now understood that these were not random splashes of color but part of their communication system. To her eyes, it was all the colors of the rainbow—except red.

The pattern reminded her of Quiet Painter.

"I'm sorry for all the loss," she said. In addition to Honest Editor, Quiet Painter was indeed damaged beyond repair, as was a robot that had helped SD in the Rejuvenation Region,

Explosive Healer. There were others, too.

"I am certain they would agree that their sacrifice was a small price to pay for global improvements," Disto said with a somber lilt.

Ruby wasn't sure that was true. She didn't think most people were that altruistic—Disto was providing a platitude to make her feel better. But again, these were robots, not people. Even though when she talked to them, she could easily convince herself that she was talking to people. She continuously had to remind herself that she wasn't. That they weren't people.

AT was next to her, slightly deflated in a way that indicated he was tired and trying to relax. He had been silent for a while.

"AT, will you be going back to your region?" Ruby asked.

"Eventually," he replied. "I want to attempt some more repairs before I do."

"And it's time for you to go home, too, Ruby," Disto said.

Ruby nodded vigorously. She couldn't agree more.

"I don't know how I'm going to explain this."

"Well, you sent your message. So, ideally when you return, they will already be aware of your situation."

"Yes, but it's not going to be that simple. There are going to be *a lot* of questions. I'll probably be forced to return to Earth. For all I know, my uncles are already there. Right before I left, we were supposed to return, anyway..."

Ruby had previously explained the situation to Disto and her other friends. She wasn't certain they entirely understood. She wasn't certain *she* entirely understood anymore. Maybe she had been acting like a spoiled brat. Her uncles cared about her, and she up and left without *really* saying goodbye. It hurt her every time she thought about her uncles finding out she'd left. The amount they must've worried, the sleepless nights they must have had. It killed her.

At the same time, now that she was here, she could save them. Her uncles always tried to get her to find the lesson within every mistake, but she was confused as to what type of lesson she should learn here.

Don't steal a ship and run away, but also if you do, you just might go on the adventure of a lifetime, come away with definitive knowledge that humans weren't alone in the universe, *and* have the opportunity to save a lot of lives?

What did Disto say about sacrifice? Is that what this was?

"Why don't you come with me?" Ruby asked.

Disto and AT looked at each other, likely attempting to parse which 'you' Ruby meant.

"By 'you,' I meant both of you. If I go back, with no robots, I'm likely going to be taken for a crazy lunatic. But if you come with me, they'll know I'm not lying."

AT sat up and inflated a smidge. "I'd like to go," he said.

Ruby watched Disto's chassis run through a myriad of colors as he processed the idea.

"Disto?"

"While I am thrilled that AT here is able to greet this unexpected offer with enthusiasm, I…"

Disto looked down at his chassis.

"Are you worried about your components holding up?"

"That's part of it. But… my programming…" He aimed his face-screen directly at Ruby. To Ruby, it was like looking deep into someone's eyes and sensing a deeper meaning. And miraculously, she understood.

"Well, we never did get an answer to my DNA and your lost storage. We're not even sure that I was the right species that SD was supposed to collect."

She waited for Disto to catch on. When she didn't see the light of recognition, she continued:

"There are so many species on Earth. Come back with us and you'll see for yourself. You can continue your search there in person. Or… in robot. I mean, instead of bringing samples back here."

"Ah," Disto said cheerfully. "Yes, that makes perfect sense. It is an extension of my mission to join you. In that case, I will join you. I will need to bring some spare components, but I will be ready shortly."

"Well, when can we leave?" Ruby asked. "I actually, um…"

"Yes?" AT and Disto said in unison.

"I really want to be home for my birthday." Ruby surprised herself by saying this out loud.

AT's face-screen lit up and then softened, "One thing... I must participate in the repair efforts, first. The Agency of Restoration, along with the Resource Allocation Agency, Reclamation and Recycling Division, have contacted all nearby Technicians to assist. I have been given the assignment to repair Austere Agent."

Ruby asked, "Are you sure that's a good idea?"

"He is damaged. I must try to repair him."

"Why you?" Ruby asked.

"I requested this assignment. I was involved in his damage. It should be me who tries to repair him," AT said. "I will go check on him now, and then we can make preparations to leave upon my return."

AT left Disto and Ruby alone. Ruby could feel Disto's visual sensors trained on her, so she asked a simple, "What? Are you surprised that AT is off to fix up that annoying Agent, too?"

Disto rolled back and forth with his head tilted down. He was rubbing his appendages together. He was clearly fidgeting.

"No, it's not that," he said. Then he asked in a low voice, "Where you're from is there... history?"

Ruby laughed, "Of course there is, Disto. Lots of it."

Disto's external chassis turned went from yellow to a rich purple. Ruby assessed that he was clearly excited about the concept of alien history. He tilted his head, "Knowing how interesting you are, Ruby, I can't begin to calculate how interesting Bio—*human*—history must be. Tell me all of it. Start at the beginning."

Ruby giggled, first at Disto's excitement and then at herself and her own attitude towards all the history classes she was required to take and how every single one of them bored her senseless. If it wasn't technological history, or didn't involve watching old movies or TV shows, she had no interest.

"All of it? The beginning? Disto, that's a lot of history—

and I'm not sure I know much of it, let alone everything. Like, there are a few thousand years of recorded human history... there were different groups of people who fought each other for resources... yeah, I don't know where to start..."

"Start with what you know?"

Ruby remembered taking a class on the history of human exploration into space. That kept her interest, and she remembered most of it.

"I guess I know a lot about when humans started to leave Earth and go out into our solar system. And I know about the history of Astroll 2, the space station where I live."

Ruby then explained some interesting facts about the lunar and Mars colonies, and Astroll 1, the station that wasn't, and Disto said, "All of these Bios—these humans—involved in these activities sound very different from you. Are you considered... abnormal?"

Ruby smirked and shrugged, "You know, Disto, I think that's subjective. But if you ask my uncles, then yes."

Ruby could tell that Disto didn't fully understand this answer, but he didn't say anything, so she continued.

Until AT interrupted their history lesson. He entered the room with a grim look on his face-screen that Ruby immediately recognized.

"What is it?" She asked.

"It's Austere Agent." AT said, "He's missing."

> Ambitious Technician <

"What do you mean missing?" Ruby asked.

Disto accelerated forward, "Yes, explain. How does one lose an inert robot?"

AT said, "I was examining Austere Agent's damaged joint mechanism, along with a group of other inert robots. I left the room momentarily to log into a console to see if the detailed specifications of this joint matched. When I returned, he was gone. Several robots are missing, 12 to be exact, including him. We submitted a general request for help from the Core. There is no division of any agency tasked with handling such an event."

Ambitious Technician knew that this was his fault. He didn't want to say more and worry Ruby, but he was afraid that a missing Austere Agent was extremely bad. Like Austere had said earlier, agents were everywhere. They were involved in every line, so it was impossible to guess what he could be up to or the power he could have. And if some unknown entity stole these robots, it could be even worse.

This problem was more than a Technician was programmed to handle. AT knew that, but also felt completely responsible. Even though he did nothing wrong, he should have... he wasn't sure what he should have done. He had replayed the event several times in the tics since and he was performing his function.

Ruby stood up and began to pace, "Well, we can still leave, right? They'll find him. AT, you don't need to stay just because of this."

"Ruby..." AT began, "I think I must stay until my tasking is complete. You will have to return to your home with Disto and without me.

AT observed Ruby's facial muscles contort and deflate. She wasn't pleased to hear this.

AT watched as her face did not improve a moment later when the ambient light in the room flickered and was accompanied by a tone that even AT found irritating.

"What's that?" Ruby asked.

AT's programming recognized it instantly, but Disto was the one who said, "It's a planetary-wide signal. It looks like no one will be leaving."

"The planet is on lockdown," AT added.

"This whole place is trying to prevent me from getting home," Ruby said. AT couldn't help but feel responsible for the situation.

"Ruby, I'm so sorry," AT said.

Disto produced a series of short beeps that indicated weariness. He said, "Let me escort you to your quarters, Ruby.

You've done enough. It's your turn to rest and be safe."

AT still wasn't an expert in Bio expressions, but Ruby exhibited the same weariness as Disto. Disto's chassis had slowly crept to more than four threets… so he was easy to read. Ruby was harder to read, but if her chassis could change color, it would certainly be between four and five, indicating clear unhappiness with the situation.

AT called after them, "I'm going to help! I will fix this, Ruby!"

Ruby shook her head and called back to him, "It's not your fault, AT. Really. It's okay."

They left AT alone in the room.

It was not okay, it was broken. "I'm a technician. I fix things. I'll fix this," AT said to himself.

> Ruby <

It had been hours since Location Zero had been on lockdown. Lockdown apparently meant that every room required a code to enter, all nonessential occurrences were halted, and most devastatingly, no one could leave the planet. So, Ruby sat in her quarters with her uncomfortable, stabby pillow, a pile of a crunchy substance the robots claimed met her description of 'chips,' salsa-flavored mush, and Pippa.

She had asked Disto if there was any way she could help, but he responded with a firm no.

"I'm sorry, Ruby, but I don't even know what has necessitated the lockdown. I don't know if it's related to our recent activity in the Hall of Templates, if it has to do with Austere Agent, or something else entirely. Until I know more, for your own safety, please stay here," he said.

"But I've helped you before, and I know I can now. There must be something I can do," she pleaded.

"Ruby, neither of us can know who can do what until we've identified the problem. Please let me go do that. I will return when I have more information."

Ruby couldn't argue with that. Maybe she could help,

maybe she couldn't, and not knowing anything about what was going on certainly was not a path to success of any kind.

So, she attempted to follow Disto's final request to her and relax. Or tried to attempt to relax. Ruby did not excel at relaxing. Add on the thoughts that she couldn't put aside: her family was in danger, and while she was here, she was powerless to do anything. *How could doing nothing be so fatiguing?*

"Pippa?" she asked eventually.

"Yes, Ruby?" Pippa responded.

"Are you still in contact with Invisible Scout?"

"We have not exchanged messages in more than a day. But I would not say I am not in contact with him."

"I wonder if he knows what's going on. Can you ask?"

"Certainly I can try…"

Before anything else was said, a new, odd sound came from above Ruby's bed. It was a light scratching that Ruby had never heard before. She looked up at the source of the sound and wondered if this was only audible in her quarters or if this was another planetary-wide alert.

It wasn't emanating at all, she discovered. What looked like a sharp knife poked through the ceiling and began tracing out a metal circle, carving a hole.

Ruby gasped, startled, and dashed out of her bed. She pointed her communicuff at the ceiling. "Pippa. Analysis."

Pippa said, "Something is carving a hole in the ceiling."

Ruby almost responded with snark, but was more focused on getting out of her room. She headed for the door when she heard something plop onto her bed. She looked behind her, and whatever made the plop sound was emitting a cloud of yellow smoke. The smoke spread quickly, and before she knew it, she collapsed in a fit of coughs.

Pippa exclaimed, "Ruby! Initiating emergency proto…"

That was the last thing Ruby heard Pippa say before everything went black.

Chapter 28

> Ruby <

Ruby woke up to more coughing. Her throat was dry and raw. She opened her eyes slowly. There was nothing to see. She was in a pitch-black room, lying on a cold floor.

Immediately she got up and began feeling the area around her. The ceiling was higher than she could reach or jump, and she felt nothing on the floor. One wall had an outline of what could have been the shape of a door, but it had no handle nor a way to pull on it, and kicking it did nothing. She felt around to the next wall and found it had no discernible features. It was blank. Another wall, blank. And the last one... covered in buttons. She pressed several, but nothing happened.

She sat on the floor, knees to chest and arms wrapped around them. She would not let herself hyperventilate or lose control. There was an explanation for this.

One thing repeated in her head.

Where. Am. I?

"The famous Ruby has been re-activated!" A booming voice came from somewhere she couldn't pinpoint.

But she recognized the voice. She said to herself, "Austere Agent."

It sounded like his voice was coming from all around her. "Bingo! While you were inactive, I took the liberty of downloading some information from your friend. Including your dictionary! You Bios have quite an entertaining and expressive vocabulary. It must make interfacing… a confusing experience."

"Where are you?" Ruby asked through clenched teeth.

Austere Agent responded, "I've upgraded. I thought that deactivation would be the worst thing that ever could happen to me, but turns out being remade does wonders!"

It was unsettling to Ruby hearing a robot talk in a way that was…so human. Especially a robot with such negative intentions.

"What do you want?" Ruby asked plainly.

Austere Agent's voice began to go in and out, changing pitch dramatically and spazzing into his native language for a word or two and then repeating it in Ruby's tongue. "Simple. I want you *gone*, Ruby Palmer."

"Then let me leave! The lockdown is because of *you, isn't it?* That's the only reason I can't get off the planet!"

"Remember when I told you that agents had wireless communication functions? I know that you were going to take Dysfunctional Historian and Average Technician to the rest of your Bios."

"Those aren't their names," Ruby said, breathing heavily with her brows angled downwards.

Austere Agent continued, "I can't risk anymore disorder. Since you've been here, you've jeopardized the integrity of our systems. Systems that…"

"Systems that were broken! Systems that I helped fix!"

"Systems that we've had in place for longer than your entire existence," Austere Agent finished his rant.

"I promise I only wanted to help you. All of you. But there were data corruptions in your very—"

"That is none of your concern!" It was Austere's turn to deliver an interruption. His voice was filled with a glitchy sounding low bass note, and it boomed all around Ruby, vibrating through her shoes. "You will not take robots to your planet! You will not do anything further! You must be reprogrammed!"

Her heart stopped. "But... but reprogramming is for robots... how would you..."

"Here's the itinerary," Austere Agent said, "You will sit here and ponder your past actions while I conclude my research on the system of systems that is a Bio and make preparations for you to be reprogrammed. When I am ready, I will provide another sedative toxin, extract your body from this chute, and finish the procedure.

"You can't do that!" Ruby was back on her feet yelling into the darkness. "I can't be 'reprogrammed!' I'm not like you! This isn't... this isn't logical!" She shouted, hoping her use of the word 'logic' would make him take pause.

Austere Agent did audibly pause, as evidenced by the soft tone she heard next. But he said, "I liked being remade. I predict, with high certainty that you will like it, too. I'll be back soon, Ruby Palmer. Don't go anywhere." He begun to make a series of tones that sounded like a modulated, demented sort of laugh. "I recently learned that that is a joke because you *cannot* go anywhere. Most robots were never programmed with the ability to make a joke, let alone a good one. I was one of those robots, but I've been improved. See you soon, Ruby Palmer."

"Wait!" she shouted. "Hold on!"

But there was no response. No tones, clicks, beeps, chimes, or anything else. He was gone.

Ruby paced, not having any ideas regarding what she could do. She kicked the wall, knowing that it wouldn't help.

Ruby let her arms and hands hang limp, and she slumped to the floor, sighing dejectedly.

"Ruby," Pippa said in the lowest volume setting.

"Pippa! I thought you'd been disabled!"

Pippa muttered, "I've been hiding. Ruby, I'm scared. I pretended to be deactivated so that he wouldn't remove me from you and destroy me. But he opened me up and looked inside..."

"I'm scared too, Pippa. But we're going to figure this out. Is there anything that you can think of to get us out of here?"

Pippa was silent. Ruby hoped that meant she was taking action. Calculating, or processing, or whatever it was that happened within her core processor. "No, I'm not detecting any signals."

Ruby took a deep breath. She needed to think logically about this. "Okay. Let's start from the top. Where are we? Do you know where we are?"

"No, Ruby. There is not enough ambient illumination to make an analysis of the room."

"Well, were you active when we were brought here? Can you make an educated guess based on our movement?"

"Also no. To pretend I was deactivated, I had to remain inactive. I was not recording data. Without a network connection, I'm not even sure how much time has elapsed."

Ruby went over everything that Austere Agent said in her mind, which was not easy given she was also working very hard to keep fear from taking over. Then it hit her.

She exclaimed, "A chute! He said we're in some sort of chute! Do you have any idea what that could mean?"

Ruby waited for Pippa to take the moment she needed to calculate. "I have accessed the map of Location Zero I downloaded to local memory from Scout. The term 'chute' describes... a lot of places."

"Disposal chutes?" Ruby asked. "I remember Disto talking about disposal chutes that connected to the recycling centers."

"Yes, there are many."

"Hmmm," Ruby was doing her thinking out loud now. "I don't know how long I was asleep, but they wouldn't have taken me far, right? It makes sense to put me in the one nearest my quarters."

"There is one that is located immediately below your quarters, Ruby, with access in the adjacent hallway."

"Okay, so let's assume that's where we are. How do we get out?"

Pippa was silent. Ruby waited patiently. But Pippa was still silent.

"Pippa?"

"Ruby?"

"How do we get out of here?"

"I do not have that information."

It's one step forward, two steps back with this one. "Pippa, can you project the map as a holo-image?"

"I have been this entire time," Pippa said.

Ruby smacked her forehead with her hand. Holo-images needed at least a little ambient light to work with. They didn't work in pitch black darkness. She knew that.

"Ok, then describe to me what's on the map. In as much detail as possible. I'll try to picture it."

As Pippa explained, Ruby tried very hard to keep a representative image in her mind, using her finger to draw in the air, not that she could see her finger, either, but she could feel it, and that was enough.

"There! Back up. What was that you just said?"

"I said 'and the horizontal lift' when you said 'There!'"

"That's it," Ruby said. "This chute is more than a chute. It's part of the lift system, and it's connected to the recycling center itself. Do we know how to operate it? If we can get to the center…"

"I will analyze the data I have downloaded from this portion of Location Zero's information system. It is limited, but I'll see what I can find," Pippa responded. And then, "The buttons on the wall are part of an emergency system. In case any robot found itself accidentally in a chute. I do not have the instructions on how to operate it."

"What if I randomly pressed them? Something is bound to work? Aren't emergency systems supposed to be easy? In case someone is panicking?"

"Do robots panic?" Pippa asked. Ruby had to think about that one. *Did they?*

Pippa continued, "A robot from the correct qualifying line would be able to operate this, even with no illumination."

"But what if another robot found itself in the chute?" Ruby countered, trying to prove to herself that she should be able to push enough buttons the same as an unprogrammed or unqualified robot would.

"Robots are not random," Pippa said.

"What does that have to do with anything?" Ruby asked.

"You said, 'what if I randomly pressed them.' A robot wouldn't press buttons randomly. They would—"

"—press them in a pre-defined sequence," Ruby caught on and finished Pippa's thought. "A simple sequence. Quick, Pippa, what are some number sequences we know?"

"Many, Ruby. There are geometric sequences, triangular sequences… There is the Bell Sequence, the Fibonacci sequence…"

"Nothing complicated," Ruby said. "If it's for an emergency, it's got to be simple."

"What about the sequence of prime numbers?" Pippa offered. "I have noticed a… a preoccupation with those special numbers."

"Let me try it." Ruby felt her way back to the button covered wall and began to feel out the buttons. She counted them, there were 41. *A prime number*, Ruby noted. *Maybe Pippa is on to something…*

"Ok, the first prime numbers are 2," Ruby pressed the second button as she said the number. "3," she pressed the third.

"5," Pippa called out, trying to be helpful.

"I know, I know all of them," Ruby said. "Well, not *all* of them, but certainly up to 41."

She continued to feel and press buttons, calling out the numbers as she did. "7, 11, 13, 17, 19, 23, 29, 31, 37, and 41," she said. "There!"

Nothing happened. Ruby sank to the floor.

"Well, that was a bust," she said. "Any other ideas?"

"You forgot one," Pippa said.

Ruby replayed the prime number sequence in her head. "No, I didn't. I got them all."

"I meant, you forgot 'one', as in, the number one."

"One is not a prime," Ruby said.

When Pippa didn't respond, Ruby said, "Pippa?"

"I cannot debate this with you, Ruby. It will... be damaging. So I will pose it as a question. Forget what prime numbers are to you. To the robots, would they consider one a prime number?"

Ruby wanted to talk this through but was also very aware that Austere Agent could be back any minute so now was not the time.

"Fine. I'll press 'one.'"

The chute began to move.

"Perfect! Pippa, I love you!"

"My emotion module is limited so I cannot express the same level of emotion, Ruby. But I am quite pleased that my analysis helped you."

Ruby laughed, "Helped *us*, you mean! Now let's hope this takes us out of here so we can find Disto and AT and tell them everything!"

> Ruby <

The lift stopped abruptly, knocking Ruby back to the floor.

"Pippa, where are we?" she asked as she stood up, instinctively dusting herself off.

Pippa didn't get a chance to answer. Instead, a voice that made Ruby's stomach sink surrounded her. "You're at the Reclamation and Recycling primary facility," said Austere Agent. "You didn't think that simply a change in physical location would prevent me from finding you? I am... everywhere. I am Location Zero."

"It's actually quite convenient," he continued. "Since we are going to 'recycle' you. That is what re-programming is, after all. Using the same structure to host a new instruction set."

The door started to open inwards, anchored at the bottom, like the lowering of a plank. Ruby made sure to be out of the way as it extended. She could see into the room beyond. Robots were hovering over conveyor belts, and there were two she didn't recognize at the doorway, with a cart in between them. She looked for someone she recognized and there was no one. One robot resembled Fastidious Mechanic, but it wasn't him... maybe another of his line.

"Pippa," she said in the lowest volume she could achieve. Ruby was certain that Austere Agent could still hear here, but she didn't have much of a choice in her methods of communication with Pippa.

"Ruby, I have a connection," Pippa said. "...and Scout is trying to contact me... he says he can help get us out if... if we'll take him with us."

"Sure, of course, I don't care," Ruby responded. "How do we get out of this?"

"Ruby, Scout says to use logic. Break his logic."

What the heck does that mean? I can't even see him... but then Ruby figured out Scout was referring to the Agent's argument and having a logical, or not so logical, argument with the disembodied robot.

"Austere Agent," Ruby said into the room, "Why do I need to be reprogrammed?"

"It's simple. All robots follow their programming. You are not a robot and all non-robots do not follow... robots are programmed."

"I am not a robot."

"Correct. But you can still be programmed."

"Not if you follow your own logic, Austere Agent."

Ruby smiled, hoping she had him, "Someone is either a robot or not a robot, correct?"

"That is correct."

"Robots are programmed."

"Also correct."

"And so not-robots are...?"

"...not programmed."

"You've got it. If A then B. If not A, then not B."

Austere Agent let out an unpleasant sound.

"Now open up and let me out of here."

The door had stopped halfway, letting in enough light for Ruby to see her way out. Ruby grabbed the edge and hoisted herself up, catching her arm on the side. The edge had a sharp corner and caught the sleeve of her jacket, ripped through it and also tore through her skin.

"Ow!" she said and held her other hand over it as she jumped down into the room, landing, not gracefully, on her feet.

Right about then the main entrance swished open, and Disto, followed by AT, rushed in. "You were right, AT," Disto was saying.

The other robots barely glanced in their direction.

"You're hurt!" was the first thing AT said when he was close to Ruby.

"It's just a scratch," she said. "I'm fine."

"No, no, let me," he said. "I'm a technician. I fix things."

"You've never fixed a Bio before," Ruby countered.

"True, but I can... you're leaking."

"No, look, it's already stopped bleeding. It was just a little."

"What happened?" Disto asked.

"It was Austere Agent. He wanted to reprogram me. But I think we... well, I'm not 100% sure, but I think he's stuck in a computational loop. Someone else can clean up the mess."

Chapter 29

> Ruby <

Ruby stood in front of the lift to her ship. Well, SD's ship. A camera was trained on her, and a newscaster was by her side.

"And your last words are?"

"Last for now, you mean. Not like, *last last*."

"Of course. Words that are your last on this planet specifically."

Ruby wanted to come up with an incredibly meaningful statement. All that she could think of were ancient movie lines. They may have sounded cheesy to her, but Ruby knew that these robots had never seen any movies, so the words would be new to them. Maybe even inspiring. "I'll be back," kept coming to mind. She didn't want to say it because she wasn't sure if it was true, and she knew that many robots would take it as a literal promise.

She looked over at Disto and AT, who both indicated that they had nothing useful to offer.

SD was already on the ship, prepping for departure.

Instead, Ruby went with simple honesty, "I'm glad I could have helped. I'll miss this place. I hope to come back someday."

It was true. She was not the same person as when she arrived. She knew more. Her brain was open to new things. She was more curious than ever. She wanted answers.

"Thank you once again, Ruby Palmer. From all of Location Zero."

The light that had been trained on her switched off, and Ruby could instantly feel the temperature drop five degrees or more. She wiped the sweat off her brow with her upper arm.

The newscasting robot was efficiently packing up his equipment and almost tripped on the boxes of stuff that Disto and AT were still planning to load onto the ship.

"Are you guys ready?" Ruby asked of her traveling companions.

"Yes, once we get this onboard," replied Disto.

"What's in there?" Ruby inquired.

"Spare parts, mostly. But the more important question is: Are you ready, Ruby?"

Ruby looked around at the hallway that was her first sight of Location Zero. Robots went about their business, passing them and not giving them a second glance.

The walls, splattered here and there with markings that the robots understood—but Ruby still needed translation help with—felt comfortable and alive. Maybe Ruby would take up painting when she got back to Astroll 2.

She was ready but also a little sad at leaving this unique and interesting place.

"Yes. But I'll be honest… I'm worried my uncles are going to be mad at me."

Before anyone said anything to that, SD emerged from the lift.

"Everything is ready," he declared.

Since they stormed the kiosks of the Hall of Templates, SD had mostly returned to his old self. *Mostly, but something is still off,* Ruby thought. Ruby had expressed her condolences at the loss of Explosive Healer.

"Except…"

"Except my ship is still in pieces, I know."

Some of *Apple Pi* had been reassembled, but not the entire ship. Without *Apple Pi*, SD's ship would have to dock directly, or they would need to find some other way to deliver Ruby to

Astroll 2.

"Look, once we get there, I'm sure they can send another mini-R-pod to get me. To get us. Easy peasy."

"And I will leave my ship in an automated standby mode."

"Exactly. This will be fine. Let's get this stuff loaded and go. Before they all forget who I am," Ruby joked, knowing the robots probably wouldn't get it.

Back at Astroll 2...

> At the Hub <

The Hub, the largest room on Astroll 2, was nearly full. Of course, on a small space station such as Astroll 2, word of a missing person spread, and everyone became attached to the story. Everyone knew Ruby Palmer on the station, and at her memorial service, everyone who could, came to pay their respects.

Ruby's Uncles were in the Nook, and her young cousin Sebastian, face red from crying when they finally told her she wouldn't be coming back, stood nearby with friends.

For those who couldn't make the memorial service in person, it was going to be broadcast station-wide.

But near the front of the room was Milo Jenkins and his teammates, who came to support him. Innogen Wilkens-Szklarski, known as Inny, was also there with her parents. She had colored her blond hair dark to honor the friend she looked up to like an older sister.

Dr. Rush Guerrero wasn't present, but he had sent words of condolences to Ruby's uncles from his ship en route to Earth.

Robt Plampton was there, too. He also stood at the Nook. In front of the microphone that carried his voice through the room and the station.

"Ruby Palmer," he began. Not only was his voice picked up

and carried, but his video image was, too. There were several large screens on the walls of the Hub, so if you didn't have a front row seat, you were guaranteed to see. Robt Plampton's image was on all of them. The green walls that were in the Nook were replaced with an image of a smiling Ruby on the background of the video screens.

"I want to thank all of you who have come to pay their respects and to honor this brave person. Many of you have already reached out to Blake and Logan, longtime colleagues here on Astroll 2 and Ruby's uncles and sponsor. I'm going to turn the podium over to them. Stick around for station announcements at the end."

With that, Uncle Logan stepped to the podium in the Nook. His usually joyful face was the exact opposite, and looking at him now, it was hard to imagine what he looked like when he smiled. Blake stood by his side with his arm linked around Logan's, almost as if he was holding him up.

"You should go first," Logan whispered to Blake, a whisper that was picked up by the microphone and broadcast to all.

"No, we talked about this. You start."

Both of their eyes were red and swollen, details also picked up and broadcast.

"Ruby came to live with us when she was five, shortly after her mother passed away," Logan began. "She was always ornery, and hardly anything she did surprised us." At this memory, one side of Logan's mouth turned up in a weak smile.

"But she never..."

The screens on the walls, and throughout Astroll 2 crackled with interference. Logan stopped to look at them. Everyone in the Hub stopped looking at Logan in the Nook and turned to look at the screens. But not only in the Hub. Every place, be it a room, computer, tablet, communicuff, or other device with a screen, even ones that had previously been dormant, came to life at nearly the same instant.

Not only on Astroll 2. Depending on the distance from Astroll 2, screens all over the solar system: on Titan, on ships in-between planets and asteroids and stations and moons, on

Mars, on the Moon, and on Earth herself a few minutes later—every screen known to humankind came to life.

And when the interference cleared, they all displayed the same image: Ruby Palmer. It wasn't a still image, however. It was a video image.

The first thing Ruby did was blink. The second thing she did was smile, a little sheepishly. The third thing she did was open her mouth to speak.

"Hi Uncle Blake, Uncle Logan. I truly hope you weren't too worried when I didn't show up on Titan. I'm okay, though. It's a long and unbelievable story, and I'll tell you all the details later. But I'm about 54 light-years from home. On an alien planet full of, get this... full of robots!"

She paused, presumably understanding that her uncles would need a moment to take this all in. But certainly not knowing that every other human in the solar system was also going to need a moment as well.

"I promise I'm okay. This message is brief because we wanted to test it out and see if it was even going to work. There are instructions on how to download a return message to the drones. Those will get downloaded to Astroll 2's computer automatically. I set that up.

"I really am okay. I can't tell you how sorry I am. I'll see you soon, and... I love you guys. A lot."

The video screens along the walls of the Hub reverted to an image of Ruby's uncles, with eyebrows raised, jaws slack, and mouths open. In fact, the whole human race might have had nearly the same look, and everyone who could look out a window or telescope did so to find the drones.

That was the day everything changed for humanity.

* * *

What's next for Ruby and her robot friends? Grab book three:
Silly Insane Humans

Robots, Robots Everywhere!

Acknowledgements and Words From the Author

Thank you for reading *Robots, Robots Everywhere!* I hope you enjoyed it and are looking forward to the next novel in the series!

Once again, I must thank my family who are somehow able to tolerate the fact that writing is something I *must* do.

Next, I have to thank everyone who loved Book 1 in The Robot Galaxy Series, *Crazy Foolish Robots,* and provided encouragement to continue! That's a lot of people. Along with those folks, I need to thank my beta readers who always provide the most helpful feedback: Dora, Anna, Ryan, Clay, Duff, and Linda. My editor, Carolani, also deserves a special shout-out as she continues to help me remember that humans have emotions and that's pretty important to show in a book, even one with a lot of robots.

To ensure you stay updated on book releases:

Join my mailing list at: **https://adeenamignogna.com**

Twitter: **https://www.twitter.com/adeena**

Facebook:
https://www.facebook.com/AdeenaMignognaAuthor

Thank you once again, wonderful reader, and I hope you're looking forward to Book 3, Silly Insane Humans, as much as I'm looking forward to getting it into your hands!

With deepest appreciation,
Adeena

Robots, Robots Everywhere!

Printed in Great Britain
by Amazon

43886317R00121